For the Love of Blood

Jamel Mitchell

Lock Down Publications and Ca$h Presents
For the Love of Blood
A Novel by *Jamel Mitchell*

For the Love of Blood

Lock Down Publications
Po Box 944
Stockbridge, Ga 30281

Visit our website @
www.lockdownpublications.com

Copyright 2022 by Jamel Mitchell
For the Love of Blood

All rights reserved. No part of this book may be reproduced in any form or by electronic or mechanical means, including information storage and retrieval systems without permission in writing from the publisher, except by a reviewer who may quote brief passages in review.
First Edition April 2022
Printed in the United States of America

This is a work of fiction. Names, characters, places, and incidents either are products of the author's imagination or are used fictitiously. Any similarity to actual events or locales or persons, living or dead, is entirely coincidental.

Lock Down Publications
Like our page on Facebook: Lock Down Publications @
www.facebook.com/lockdownpublications.ldp
Book interior design by: **Shawn Walker**
Edited by: **Kiera Northington**

Jamel Mitchell

Stay Connected with Us!

Text **LOCKDOWN** to 22828 to stay up-to-date with new releases, sneak peaks, contests and more…
Thank you.

Submission Guideline.

Submit the first three chapters of your completed manuscript to ldpsubmissions@gmail.com, subject line: Your book's title. The manuscript must be in a .doc file and sent as an attachment. Document should be in Times New Roman, double spaced and in size 12 font. Also, provide your synopsis and full contact information. If sending multiple submissions, they must each be in a separate email.

Have a story but no way to send it electronically? You can still submit to LDP/Ca$h Presents. Send in the first three chapters, written or typed, of your completed manuscript to:

LDP: Submissions Dept
Po Box 944
Stockbridge, Ga 30281

DO NOT send original manuscript. Must be a duplicate.

Provide your synopsis and a cover letter containing your full contact information.

Thanks for considering LDP and Ca$h Presents.

Jamel Mitchell

Thank You's

First and foremost, all praises are due to Allah. I would like to thank my Queen... Mommy. My beautiful sister Jameela. My three precious boss babies, my nieces Jamey, Jordyn, and Empress. My wonderful and Shawt m smart nephew King. Can't forget the reason that I still strive: My three Kingz, Tah'Keem, Ke'mante and Ethan. Daddy loves you with every ounce of love in my soul. Thank you for having patience when I am too difficult to be around. You are ttyl truly my rock. Without the love and support of my familia this book would have been impossible.

...To all my niggas that inspired me to write this story... Chace Miller (R.I.P.), Hakeem Brown (R.I.P.), Torien "Weezy" Williams and Robert "Squeeze" Veltri (R.I.P.). You'll forever be loved and missed. This book is dedicated to your memory.

...To my niggas that supported me through my daily struggle. To my brothers Blair Templeman, Dewaine Jones ... All I can say is thank you my G. What's understood doesn't need to be explained. Know that this growth half belongs to y'all. I remember nights when I saw disappointment in your faces, yet you niggaz never gave up on me. On gang, I will love y'all forever for that.

Sach Moe ... Skino ... Braheem, I can't even explain the loyalty that we were blessed with. My day one trench brothers. I love you niggaz till the day Allah calls me up. You men showed me that loyalty is a real thing. You showed me that blood only makes you related, loyalty makes you *family*. Y'all always been there even when the odds were stacked against us. Real nigga shit.

...To all my goons behind the G-wall, keep it live and remain *100*. Charlie B ... Jed ... Al Gutta ... Blizzy B. Rollack ...

For the Love of Blood

Gun Smoke ... Shake... B-More Dink ... Murda Montana ... Marco ... Marco ... Ping Pong ... Lor ... Dravo... Ned … AD ... Lavonte ... Gun Hill Chima ,,, Courtland Ave Josh ... Zach ... C Murda. If l forgot you my apologies it's all love though. I have learned something about myself through each of you. I appreciate your daily support and push.

To the women that support their men that's behind the G-wall. Respect when respect due. Good looking Virginia "Ginger" Veltri for your constant support and advice. There were lots of nights I wanted to give up but you made sure, for the love of the homies and my family, that I to continued to strive and *that* I have done. Thank you very much.

Lynitrah Woodson, first of all, you were one of the best things that happened to a nigga, so I have to give you your love and respect. Your inspiration pushed me to become not only a man but a great man. Loving you made me want to be more; made me want to be great. I was the luckiest man in the world when we was one, and still I stand very grateful of your presence in my life. Thank you for the ambition and for believing in my education and success. You are a very beautiful person, inside and out.

Last but not least, the mothers of my children ... Naeshia "Keya" Gravely and Tanjauah "Nay Nay" Brown. I thank you Keya for being present and keeping my baby in my life. Nay Nay I know we don't get along much, but know I love y'all unconditionally.

Lastly, the hood that made me the man I am today... Courtlandt Ave, stand up!

In loving memory of Jah' Lil Kyree Clements. We love and miss you.

Jamel Mitchell

Chapter 1

Ring... Ring... Ring... Ring... The phone rang incessantly, waking Simfany out of her sleep.

"Hello?" she finally answered in a groggy voice.

"Ma, I'm locked up!" Simfany sat up, alert as soon as she heard the distant voice of her only son on the other end of the phone.

"Santana, what the fuck are you talking about?" she asked, now fully awake.

"They booked me for murder. I was—" Santana tried to explain.

"Hold on ... Hold on ... nigga, what the fuck you mean they booked you for murder?" she asked, cutting him off.

"Where are you?"

"Charleston," Santana replied in a child-like voice. Simfany shook her head.

"Damn, you don't fuckin' listen. I told you to stay out of West Virginia." Simfany sighed.

"Never mind that. I'll be down there tomorrow, omerta, baby."

"I'm good, Ma, I haven't said anything. I asked for a lawyer," Santana said with pride.

"Good, remain stable and hold your head. I'm on my way. I'll be there first thing in the morning. I love you, baby boy," she finally said.

"I love you too, pretty lady." Simfany hung up the phone and sat in bed, and she reminisced back to how the cycle began.

Nineteen years earlier

Fall 1988

It was a cold brisk day in The Bronx as Simfany made her way home from work. As she hurried down 153rd and Courtlandt Avenue, she saw the same broke ass niggaz hugging the block as usual. She shook her head and smiled. These niggas need to get a fucking life. Everybody on the corner stopped to give Simfany a silent onceover as she passed by. Simfany knew she was the center of attention as she walked by, so she slowed down and intentionally put more sway in her hips to purposely tease each dude on the corner with her 34D-26-44 Coke bottle figure. Even though it was covered from the bulky North Face coat she wore, her Puerto Rican and Black features stood out, demanding attention with ease.

"How you doing, ma?" Emilio asked as he made his way past her.

"I'm good, Emilio. How bout you?"

"Holding it down like always."

"Good to hear, be safe."

"You too, ma." Simfany turned her back to start her journey home.

"Simf, when you gone stop playing games and let me take you out? a bold voice called out from behind the crowd. She stopped and turned around.

"As soon as you stop putting your dick in these neighborhood groupies," Simfany replied, recognizing the sexy yet powerful voice of Dracula.

Cartez "Dracula" Vega was known in the hood for his hoop game. Everybody knew he was the next big thing to get in the NBA. But this all came to a screeching halt when he was booked for murder. He was accused of stabbing a man to

For the Love of Blood

death in the neighborhood. He was eventually released, on behalf of his lawyer, who demonstrated self-defense. The NBA did not want the controversy, so he was never drafted. Just that quick, Dracula lost all he had worked his whole life for. So, he fell back to the only thing he knew more than basketball...the streets. He was now a major player in the drug game in the South Bronx.

"Come here, Chula, don't act like that," Dracula called out as he approached.

"What you want, Cartez?" she asked with a smug expression.

"Damn, ma, I come in peace," he replied, raising his hands playfully to show he was unarmed.

"Let me take you. I promise, I won't bite. Lick maybe, but not bite." Simfany laughed.

"I don't got time for the bullshit, Dracula," she replied in a hushed tone. Simfany had a little crush on Dracula since their days at I.S. 162, but back then he was so occupied with all the other females in school, he paid her no attention to her. Now he was on her hard. She thought, *damn, how the tables have turned.*

"What you doing tonight?' Can I come scoop you for dinner and a movie?" Please, ma?"

Simfany contemplated whether she should accept the invitation or play him like he did her for many years. But she went against her better judgment.

"Sure," she finally answered.

"Give me some time to change out of my work clothes." Simfany said, looking down at her Duane Reade uniform.

"Shit, ma, you look fine to me. Let me go get my whip and I'll be right back. You cool with that?"

She looked at her appearance yet again, then hesitantly nodded. Dracula jogged off to retrieve his car. A few minutes later, Dracula pulled up in a brand-new, all-black Acura Legend. The sight of the car instantly made Simfany moist between her thighs. Dracula got out of the car and opened the passenger side door for Simfany.

"After you, pretty lady." Simfany got in the car as Dracula pulled off, leaving everyone standing on the corner with all eyes on them.

In the car, they looked at each other for a moment as their thoughts ran wild with anticipation. An awkward silence filled the air. Dracula spoke first.

"Why you keep stunting on me, Simf? I'm interested in getting to know you."

"You would get to know me if…never mind. I know your type, Drac. Don't forget, we grew up in the same hood, even if you forgot I exist. I know how you niggas get down," Simfany replied.

"Fuck is that supposed to mean? Don't dismiss me before you get to know me today, Simf." Simfany smiled at the nickname he gave her many years ago. She snapped out of her daze.

"Nigga, I just judge you by the bitches you keep in your company." Dracula gave Simfany a crazy look. She elaborated.

"Nigga, the bitches around you define your character. Birds of a feather flock together." Dracula was speechless.

"Then why don't you be the one to break the image?" he said in a matter-of-fact tone. She thought about what Dracula said, but quickly changed the subject.

"Since I don't know you, who are you, Mr. Vega?" Simfany asked, calling Drac by his last name. He smiled.

"You can find out, just give me the chance," Dracula replied as he looked deep into her eyes. For a second, he lost sight of everything around him…even the road.

For the Love of Blood

"Boy, you better pay attention to the road," Simfany said playfully. He gave her another once over and focused his attention back to the road. The conversation continued as he drove the rest of the way to Dallas BBQ's, a popular restaurant in lower Manhattan. What they didn't know about each other, they explored over dinner that evening. From this night on, Dracula and Simfany would be inseparable.

***

As the months passed, Dracula and Simfany built what most would call a "death do us part" relationship. Whenever you saw one, you saw the other. It was no surprise when Simfany gave Dracula the news of her pregnancy. The couple were ecstatic about giving birth to their first child.

Welcoming a son into the world made Dracula re-evaluate his position in the streets, he was financially stable enough to take care of ten families if he wanted. During the pregnancy, Dracula continued to go hard in the streets. He instilled fear in the competition and safety for his soldiers on the grind. In the process, he was grooming the next to take over if he decided to step down.

Emilio was Dracula's block lieutenant. He ran everything from the ground up. Emilio was the person who got his hands dirty. Not only was Emilio his most loyal block lieutenant, but he was also his best friend. They grew up eating free lunch together at P.S.1 and playing skelly on sidewalks. As they sat in one of their many stash spots, they started talking about the future of the game.

"You know, E, I'm thinking about getting out the game," Dracula said as he gazed out the window.

"You sure that's what you want? Are you willing to give up all this?" he asked Dracula as he pointed out the window at the empire they built together.

"I'm sure, E. I'm about to have this baby. My familia before the love of the paper, homie. You feel me?" Dracula replied, still looking over Melrose Houses.

"I'll keep shit straight, Drac, you won't have to worry about that."

"Even after all we been through, I still got your best interest at heart." E spoke of the bad blood they had only months ago.

"Shit, I would hope so, fam. A bond that is broken is a bond that never existed, my nigga." Emilio exhaled. They shook hands, and Dracula made promises to get back soon to the "Take Over" situation.

***

It was the day both Dracula and Simfany waited so patiently for. Dracula received the call that Simfany was in labor. On August 7, 1989, Simfany gave birth to a healthy baby boy in Lincoln Hospital. They named him Santana Vasquez. Dracula looked at his newborn and smiled. Allah gave him the most precious gift a life can give.

"Let me hold him, ma." Dracula reached out for his son. Santana was so small and fragile, he made sure to handle him with care. At that moment, Santana stretched his little arms and his little fist, finding his father's finger, easily wrapped around it. He looked down at his son and spoke his first words of truth.

"I swear on my heartbeat, you will never want for anything. And I promise to protect you and your mother to my dying day." Not knowing how true his statement really was,

For the Love of Blood

Dracula kissed Santana on his lips and handed him back to Simfany. He leaned over and kissed Simfany passionately.

"Thank you, my love, you have made me the happiest man in the world today. Neither one of you will need or want for anything. I can promise my life on that, pretty lady." He rose to leave, looking back at his family and his heart filled with warmth. Simfany understood the block called and he had to leave. Business had to be handled. When Dracula left, Simfany snuggled up to Santana and rocked him until he was sound asleep.

Dracula remained in the game, despite what he told Emilio. Being next in line, Emilio was furious when Dracula changed his mind to stay connected to the streets. Emilio knew he earned the position to be the boss and the loyalty he once had quickly turned to hate. Emilio despised Dracula, but still played his position. Dracula continued to feed Emilio, he was too busy showing love, he missed the signs of brewing hate. Emilio plotted Dracula's demise from that day on.

***

The year flew by, money was made, bodies were dropping, and the summer was back in full effect. Santana's one-year birthday was today and everyone in the hood was aware. Dracula had plans to do it big for his son's first birthday celebration. He decided to celebrate Santana's birthday on Melrose Day. This was a day in the community where members of the project housing came together to celebrate and represent where they lived. Usually, the festivals were the highlight of the day. This year, Santana was the person of interest. At one year of age, he was treated like hood royalty. Everyone loved him, and if they didn't, they acted like they did. The day party was a success. By nightfall, the goons came out to play on Courtlandt Avenue.

As the sun went down and drinks were consumed, egos flared, and niggas' pride was tested.

"Put a stack on it, nigga!" Drac challenged the group.

"What? Niggas scared my man gonna hit better than a fever? You niggas ain't getting no money," Drac laughed and shook his head.

"Bet then, nigga!" Wayne called out, testing Emilio's bluff.

"Drop ya bread then, nigga. No lay-lay, no pay." Emilio said as he shook the loaded dice. He let them fly four-five-six…

"C-lo nigga, give me my muthafucking money," a drunken Emilio slurred. The pot contained close to fifty-five hundred. Both Emilio and Dracula reached down to get their money. Dracula made a side blind bet that Emilio had loaded the dice. The scam was all too familiar to Dracula when they were young kids just having fun, trying to come up. Emilio reached for his money but stopped short when something caught his eye.

"Damn, that bitch bad," Emilio said out loud. Drac turned around to see who Emilio was speaking about, and the smile faded when he realized who was in his best friend's vision. Dracula stood up.

"Fuck you mean, nigga, you out of pocket." He addressed the situation the best way he felt possible. Emilio was drunk, so he spoke what was on his mind. The words flowed with ease. The sight Emilio had captured was of Simfany. He snapped out his daze seconds later.

"All I was saying was that ya bitch bad, it ain't that serious, nigga." Emilio refused to lose eye contact with Dracula.

For the Love of Blood

Everybody stopped and stared at the long-time friends. What would soon unfold would be talked about for many years.

"Miss me with that shit, son, stop looking at shit you will never have," Dracula said with confidence.

"Son, y'all niggas out here tripping, son." Wayne tried to dissolve the issue before it got out of hand. Emilio moved Wayne out of his way as he stepped closer to Dracula.

"Nah, watch out, nigga. Nobody wants that bitch, my nigga. Fuck you mean...." It was the last word Emilio got to say before Dracula punched Emilio in the face. Emilio staggered a little before he retrieved his weapon. He trained his 9mm on his friend of fifteen years. He felt nothing as he pulled the trigger, *Boc...Boc...Boc...Boc...Boc...Boc*...hitting Dracula in his chest five times. People scattered as the shots were being fired. The only people left were the block boys and Simfany.

The block boys stood by, shocked at what just took place. But they said and did nothing. They worked for Dracula, but their loyalty was to Emilio. He was the one out there with them daily, putting in work with sweat, tears and blood. For this reason alone, no one stepped up to protect Dracula from his demise. Emilio stood over Dracula, watching him gargle on his own blood, body twitching.

"You should have left when you had a chance, son," Emilio said as he squeezed two more shells into his head, silencing Dracula forever. Emilio ran off. Simfany watched in horror as she ran to Dracula's limp body and began to shake him.

"Please don't leave me, baby," she begged and cried hysterically.

"Somebody, please help me, call 9-1-1 please!" she cried out. Her plea for help seemed to fall on deaf ears. She continued to rock back and forth, talking to Dracula's lifeless body.

17

It felt as if her soul was being lifted out of her body. She couldn't breathe. She wiped her tears away and looked into his lifeless eyes again.

"I'm going to kill that nigga, baby, if that's the last thing I do. I will always love you, Cartez." She closed Dracula's eyes and continued to rock back and forth. Simfany's heart hardened as she waited for the police and ambulance to arrive. She held on to her only love until the police forced her away with guns drawn.

***

Dracula's murder was felt throughout the five boroughs. His death was felt most prominent in Melrose and Jackson Houses. At one, Santana felt the absence of his beloved father. The hood wasn't the same and business kept going as usual. There was a new king on the rise. Emilio took control of the blocks he helped build, but it wasn't easy. After Emilio killed Dracula, many men tried to murder him, but he laid his murder game down. And one by one, Emilio and his team of young bulls from North Philly played for keeps.

***

As the years crept by and Santana grew, Emilio became a household name of fear and respect. Emilio was out of town when he recognized a familiar voice. *It has been years since I last saw her and damn, she looks good,* Emilio thought as he followed Simfany through the packed club.

Simfany took in the scene of her new club, which was located on 161st and The Grand Concourse. She named it in memory of her lost love. *Vampire Life* was packed to full capacity on opening night. Simfany enjoyed the potential the club possessed, as she looked over the crowd and stared at her success. Her happiness was short-lived as her eyes fell upon Emilio approaching. *I gotta be seeing shit!* she thought as she wandered back to the night Dracula was murdered. Lost in thought, she didn't pay Emilio much attention until he grabbed her elbow and turned her around to face him.

"Can I speak with you for a minute?" Emilio asked.

"Nigga, don't put ya motherfucking hands on me," Simfany replied, walking off. Emilio ran after Simfany.

"Ma, please. This is a conversation that needs to take place. Give me five minutes and I promise, I'll leave."

"Come on, nigga." She headed to her office in the back of the club. Her office was a spacious room, with a desk in the middle of the floor. Two black leather couches were carefully placed against the maroon-colored walls. Pictures of Santana and Dracula were hung all over the room. As they made their way into the room, Emilio noticed the pictures, but it did not faze him. Emilio stood.

"Sit down, Emilio," Simfany said.

"Nah, I'm good, this won't take long." He continued, "Look Simf, I come in peace, I don't want you to fear me."

"What you mean, how am I supposed to feel? You killed my son's father. Better yet, you killed your right-hand man!" Emilio looked down in shame.

"He would have killed me, Simfany, what the fuck was I supposed to do?" he asked.

Nigga, I don't care, I wish it would have been you buried, she thought as he continued to talk. But she did ask herself, *if the tables were turned would Dracula have killed Emilio?* This was too much at once. She let her emotions get the best of her.

"To be truthful, that would have a better outcome, nigga," she said coldly. Emilio acted as if he didn't hear what she said.

19

"Please forgive me, ma. I swear, I meant no harm by the shit that took place. I was drunk and honestly don't remember what I was doing that day."

"Is that all? Because you can leave," she replied flatly.

"Bitch, that's your last time coming at me like that, I told you I come in peace. I fucked up, that I can admit and take responsibility for. But stop talking to me like I'm some kind of pussy. I am here to try to help you and Santana. But that is on you," Emilio said as he took two steps towards her, never breaking eye contact.

"My nigga, my son's father made sure I was good financially," Simfany said as she looked around at her new investment. The truth was, she was fucked financially. Simfany spent the money she had several years ago on the club. She made specific sacrifices to be where she was today. It was a dire need for the club to be a success, but she refused to tell Emilio that. Emilio wrote his number down on a piece of paper he found on Simfany's desk.

"Here's my number, if your stubborn ass need anything, call me and I got you." Be safe, ma. And again, I apologize." He turned and left Simfany alone with her thoughts. She looked at the paper on her desk and crumbled it up and threw it into the wastebasket near her desk. Tears flowed down her face, so she let them fall. She was tired of wiping the tears away.

Composing herself, she got up and made her way back into the club. Simfany was there to celebrate her grand opening and that's what she planned on doing. She thought about Dracula, but she didn't want to ruin her night, she promised herself that much.

The music blared, everybody seemed to be having a good time. *Do you know what today is…it's our anniversary…anniversary…* Tony! Toni! Toné! sang through the speakers.

For the Love of Blood

The atmosphere made Simfany smile, *maybe this wasn't a bad idea,* she told herself. The rest of the night went surprisingly smooth for Simfany. No shootings or fights in or outside the club. After the club let out, she helped with the clean up and went home satisfied.

***

"Ock, was that Drac's bitch you were talking to in the club?" one of his soldiers asked.

"Yeah. I am trying to ease shorty over a little, if you know what I mean." He smiled.

"I see you, Ock," his young nigga from Philly shouted as he dapped him up. Emilio reached for his car phone. He dialed the last known number for Simfany. The number was disconnected. A dead end. He decided to check some spots Dracula once had, still no sign of Simfany. *Fuck, I'll see shorty again. The Yitty too small*, he thought as he hit the joint in his hand.

***

Time flew by for Simfany, the club was doing good numbers and Santana was turning six. She was doing well despite the things that took place in the past. Simfany was content with life. She and Santana walked hand in hand through the cemetery. They were there to visit Dracula's gravesite. It became a regular outing around this time of year. It was also Santana's sixth birthday. Simfany would never forget how Dracula was murdered on his son's first birthday.

"Mommy, why do we always have to come see Daddy here?" Santana looked up and asked his mother.

"Because baby, Daddy went to be with God. This is all we have to remember him," she explained in the best way she could to a six-year-old.

"Mommy, did Daddy love me?" Santana asked as he looked up at his mother for answers.

"Of course, baby. Why do you ask that, Santana?" she responded, with tears forming at the corner of her eyes.

"Just asking, because I know I will always love him."

"He is looking down here every day to make sure you and mommy are okay." Santana looked towards the sky and waved, hoping his father could see him. Simfany wiped her tears away, thinking how much they needed Dracula around. Simfany missed Dracula to the point of death.

When Dracula was killed, Simfany contemplated ending her own life, but she changed her mind just as fast as the thought came to fruition. She had an obligation to Santana as well, so she pushed the thought of suicide to the end of her mind. Santana walked over to the tombstone and placed the flowers they brought down. He walked back to his mother and held her leg for what seemed like forever. Simfany squatted down and hugged Santana. Santana saw the tears in his mother's eyes and teared up himself. He reached up and wiped her tears.

"It'll be okay, Mommy, remember Daddy is looking down on us," Santana reminded her.

Simfany smiled at his innocence.

"Come on, little man, time to go. You have a birthday to enjoy." She stood up. Santana stopped after a couple steps. He took off his chain Simfany bought for his third birthday, he ran back to his father's gravesite and sat the cross down between two candles and hugged the tombstone. He made his way back toward his mother. Simfany's heart cried, she knew what would eventually happen to the gold chain, but she let it be and walked out the graveyard, hand in hand with her son. Santana wouldn't forget that day, ever. Even though he didn't get the chance to meet his father, Dracula's morals and values would always live deep inside of Santana.

Jamel Mitchell

Chapter 2

Summer 2001

"Yo, ma, what are you doing in there? I gotta go," Santana screamed as he knocked on the bathroom door.

"Nigga, if you don't stop talking like that, I'm gone punch you in your fucking mouth. I'm not ya little girlfriend, I'm your mother, Santana. Now move!" Simfany said as she made her way out the bathroom. Santana had the look of shock on his face.

"Dang, I didn't mean anything by it. I just need my hair braided before I go to the Skate Key tonight." It was Santana's twelfth birthday, and The Key was sponsoring a party for Santana. Simfany came out of pocket for it, of course.

"Sit your little ass down. All them little hoochies you got chasing you, and don't none of them know how to braid hair?" she asked. He laughed.

"Yeah, but they all say it's way too long." Simfany parted his hair in two, to give him two French braids. *Damn this little nigga's hair is too long, too long to keep fucking with it,* she thought. Santana's hair ran down to the middle of his back. Simfany grabbed the Luster's Pink lotion and greased his scalp.

"Thank you, pretty lady," Santana said as he kissed his mother's cheek. She loved when he called her that, it made her feel like the only girl in his world. It was the same way Dracula made her feel when he would say it. At that moment, she was the only queen rocking his throne, so she basked in it. She knew one day, she would have to give it up.

"You're welcome, baby, happy birthday too. Don't be down Patterson Projects tonight, bring your ass home after Skate Key lets out." She looked at him. "Santana, I'm not

25

playing with you. Don't make me fuck you up!" she said, looking Santana in his eyes. Simfany walked over to Santana and kissed him on the forehead.

"I got you, Mom, it close at two, come get me and Justice fifteen minutes before. Those dudes started shooting last week. I ain't trying to be there for all that. Oh, and can you get some chicken from the KFC on the corner before you come? You know a nigga gone be hungry."

"I'll be there, have fun and be safe please. You can eat when y'all get home."

"Ight, I love you."

"Love you too, baby boy." Simfany watched as Santana grabbed his money off the kitchen table, heading out the door. Santana had chills down her spine every time he left the house. He was just like his father was in middle school. Simfany laughed to herself, her baby boy was growing up. Santana was a splitting image of Dracula, only a shade lighter with long hair.

Simfany got up and finished the chores around the house.

***

"Damn nigga, what took you so long?" Justice asked as Santana made his way out of the building.

"I had to get my hair done, plus you know Ma Dukes be all emotional and shit," Santana replied.

"True story, she do be going hard at you. How we gone get to The Key tonight? You asked ya moms for a ride?"

"Nah, Marissa and Summer supposed to come and scoop us," he explained to Justice.

"Who they riding with?"

"Carter." Santana looked over at Justice, who was looking at him like he was crazy. Santana busted out laughing.

"What nigga, you scared Carter gone get in that ass or something?" Santana teased.

"Shit, son, you the one riding with ya girl's pops, not me. He gone kill you. I'm good," Justice replied seriously.

"Be easy, my G, here they come," Justice said, nodding at the green Expedition coming down the block. Santana dusted himself down as the truck approached. The back door came open once the car came to a halt. Santana hopped in, Justice followed suit.

"Happy birthday, Tana!" Summer yelled from the passenger seat.

"Good looking, sis," he replied as he leaned up and hugged her. He called her sis because he knew she wanted to be so much more than that. It just set that boundary for both of them. Summer could never understand why Santana fell in love with her sister, Marissa. Summer was the oldest at fifteen years old, Marissa being the youngest at thirteen. Summer was sexier but she had too much going on in the hood, so he played his distance from her on that tip. They were cool though, Summer always had Santana's back.

When she went to P.S.151 and he went to the school up the block P.S. 156, she would walk home with him. As kids, Jackson and Melrose despised each other, elementary school beef. Summer wouldn't let the Jackson kids jump him or Justice. Summer was more like his nigga than everything. He didn't look at her in that manner, even though he already knew what it was with her. Plus, that was the nigga Big E's main squeeze.

Big E was second-in-command of Va-Holla. Bogus was the head nigga. Va-Holla was a bunch of young niggas who wanted to be blood. Santana wasn't in the gang, but he fucked with them hard body, blood niggas in training as he liked to

27

call them. They went hard for what they believed in, that's what caught Santana's attention.

"How you doing, ma?" he looked over at Marissa.

"I'm good, just happy to finally see you for a change," she replied under her breath.

Santana looked up and caught eye contact with Carter in the rearview mirror. Santana cheesed for him. That made Carter smile.

"How you doing, Mr. Nunez?" Santana asked.

"Chill with all that Mr. Nunez shit. You know I hate that shit." Carter Nunez was one of the last legends left in the hood, the only one that actually escaped jail or death. He wasn't the girl's biological father, but he helped raise them from damn near birth. His brother was gunned down at a car dealership in the early 90s, leaving behind two beautiful girls. Carter took custody and took care of them like they were his own, the rest was history.

"Happy birthday though, little nigga. Son, you growing up fast. That's what's good." Carter pulled off. For the rest of the ride, Santana and Marissa caught up on lost time. Justice, Carter, and Summer just mellowed out to the infamous Hot 97.

"Make this money take this money ain't no way you can take this from me, ain 't shit funny, shake it honey, make this money, now let's get it..." G-Dep blasted through the speakers as they made their way into The Key. Santana could hear the DJ as he made his way through the metal detectors and paid for his ticket.

"It's live in The Key tonight... Bronx in the house... Got Brooklyn in the house... Queens in the house... Harlem getting down... New Yitty makes some noise... I said, New Yitty make some noise." The crowd went wild as Jose chanted over the mic.

For the Love of Blood

As Justice, Summer, Marissa and Santana made their way through the skating rink, people were still skating. On Saturday, the skating part stayed open until 9:00 pm, then the skates were turned in. Then the skating rink turned into a Kid club until 2:00 am. Justice and Santana were present almost every weekend faithfully. A lot of people knew who Santana was because his father was a hood legend in The Bronx. How he was murdered, and who murdered him would never be forgotten. Santana pulled Marissa to the side for some alone time, they sat down at the closest table located near the lockers and the bathroom.

"You know I love you, right?" Santana said as he looked into Marissa's eyes.

"I love you too, Tana, you know that. But when will we tell Carter and Simfany about our relationship?" Marissa asked in concern.

"Shit, I always was the one that was ready. So, whenever you feel as though you're ready, I'm with it. Just know I truly loved you if Carter kills me," he joked.

"Happy birthday, sexy!" She pulled him in for a kiss. She knew everybody would be looking, it was just a way to claim what was hers. Santana knew what Marissa was doing and went with the flow, he would never disrespect his shorty. Their moment was interrupted by the DJ.

"Santana, where are you? We got a birthday to celebrate, son. Come show these people how Melrose gets it poppin." The DJ was from Courtlandt Avenue, it was all hood love through the building. It was a bunch of Courtlandt Avenue representatives present that particular night, Melrose and Jackson. Santana and Marissa made their way to the DJ booth to show love to the partygoers. After all, they were there for him. As Santana and Marissa walked hand in hand, jealousy was etched over many faces. But the pair paid no mind to the unwanted attention. They made it inside of the DJ's booth, Santana hugged Jose and proceeded to the mic. He was so short, Santana had to stand on a crate to be able to see the crowd.

"First off, I wanna thank everybody that came out to celebrate my born day. Don't get shit fucked up. I know most of y'all don't give a fuck and just want to have a good time. I respect that!" the crowd laughed. "But please respect what's going on tonight. Remember, we here to have fun. Furthermore, I hear a lot of rumors about niggas who think they can beat lil' Macho in a Harlem Shake contest. Well, this what I'm gone do, whoever think they got what it takes, step up.

"You win five hundred if you can prove you're better. If Macho goes undefeated, he gets the money, so niggas better show out. But remember, no hard feelings. Mach, hold it down for the X, my G!" Santana saluted Macho before he stepped down from the crate.

That night, a dozen or so people stepped up to the challenge, both boys and girls. To make it fair, the crowd voted for the winner. Macho crushed each opponent one by one. Macho left five hundred dollars richer and his crown intact. He held it down once again for Va-Holla and his hood, Morehouse projects. The night was a success for The Key without violence. Simfany slid through and picked him and Justice up at 1:45. Marissa and Summer went home at midnight when Carter came and got them. What Santana didn't know was that in a year or so from this day, his life would change forever, facing juvenile life in somebody else's city.

***

Simfany made her way to the popcorn stand in the Magic Johnson Theatre. She was out to enjoy the day. Simfany stood

For the Love of Blood

in line waiting on her junk food. The man in front of her was talking on the phone, not paying attention as the server called for him to step up. Not wanting to continue to stand and wait on the guy, she tapped him on his shoulder to alert him that he was being called. The man turned around and Simfany instantly lost her breath. It was Emilio. She hadn't seen Emilio since the night he showed up at her club years prior. The last she heard, he moved out of town, she wasn't so sure because it was too far back to remember the reason why. Truthfully, it didn't really matter to her.

Every time she saw Emilio, her thoughts reverted back to the night she watched him stand over Dracula and squeeze the fatal shots into his head. That gave her chills still to this day. The crazy thing, though she decided to forgive him, she could never forget. Simfany wanted to leave the past behind her, she was truly ready to close that chapter in her life. Emilio looked back on the phone, but he showed no sign of recognition. He moved to the counter and ordered his food. As he waited, Simfany was called also. She also ordered and stood to the side. Emilio looked at Simfany. His eyes scanned her face, then her body. Recognition set in. Simfany was still beautiful, if not sexier.

"Excuse me, do I know you?" Emilio asked.

"How could you not? How are you doing, Emilio?" She looked at him annoyed.

"I thought that was you, damn it's been a long time. What, like seven, eight years since I last saw you?" he asked.

"Something like that. The last time, I heard you moved." She decided to be an asshole. He laughed at her.

"And leave all this money behind? Nah truthfully, the shit with Drac hit me hard. I didn't deserve those blocks, ma. I killed my man over some bullshit. When niggas young, they tend to be on some bullshit." He looked Simfany in her eyes. *I can't let shorty slide this time,* he thought.

"But I still want to help you and little man the best I can. My offer still stands. The last time I gave you my number, you never used it. So, let me get your number," he asked her. She thought about it.

"No. But go ahead and give me your number and I'll make sure to use it if I'm in need of anything," she said. Simfany had no intention of really using the number. Whether she wanted to admit it or not, she would find out how useful the number would become.

"Be patient, I'll call you. What happened to my baby father is still a sour subject. I have a lot of questions that need to be answered. So, I'll be definitely calling you soon. Do you still live in New York, or are you just visiting?" Simfany asked as she grabbed her popcorn off the counter.

"I'm back for good, been back for a while. I set up shop in Harlem. Get at me, ma, and don't be a stranger. How Santana? I bet son huge."

"Yeah, but he short as hell, he looks just like his father to the point it gives me the chills," she said, thinking about her son. Emilio said nothing. He gave her his number, then they said their goodbyes and went separate ways.

***

Simfany thought of Emilio ever since they ran into each other. What he said at the movie theater, she couldn't get out of her mind. *The last time, he blamed killing Dracula on just being drunk and he didn't mean to do it. Now his story changed to, he killed his man over some bullshit.* Simfany was lost. *I might be reading into the two comments too much. Now I'm at the point, I need to know what the fuck happened,* she thought as she reached for the phone. Yet, it was just an excuse to call Emilio. Simfany called the number he wrote down for her. The call went unanswered. She thought about leaving a message but decided against it. She tried again, still no answer. This time, she swallowed her pride and left a message with the info to reach her.

***

Hours later, and still no luck with reaching Emilio. He never called back. Two weeks went by before she heard from Emilio.

Ring ... Ring ... Ring ... Simfany looked at the caller ID, the call was listed as private. Simfany didn't answer. The caller called back immediately, and it concerned her, so she answered.

"Hello, who is this?" she asked with concern all in her voice.

"Emilio. You looking for me, you alright?" he asked. Simfany sighed, now that the fear of danger was gone. She wanted to know what happened that fatal night. She needed some kind of answers.

"Where you at?" she asked.

"I'm out on business right now, but I'll get at you once I'm free."

"Call when you're on your way. I'm ready for some answers." She let her words linger, before she hung up, leaving Emilio speechless. Over the years, Simfany learned how to conceal her emotions. She cried once the phone went dead, Simfany wiped her tears away. She had to go to her club today to see what the numbers were like. *Now I needed to go get my mind off the bullshit,* she thought. She owned the club for close to seven years. At the beginning, it was called *Vampire Life* in memory of Dracula, but recently, she changed it to *Pleasures*. Simfany was lucky she was still in business. After all the shootings, stabbings, and fights that took place in and around the club, her shit should have been shut down. She was impressed with the longevity her club endured.

***

Simfany arrived at *Pleasures* to see it packed, despite the violence it brought weekly. As she stepped into the club, the DJ had one of her favorite songs playing through the speakers.
Every little thing that we do is strictly between me and you, the freaky things that we do, is strictly between me and you .... Baaaby ....
Simfany swayed to the beat. Damn she loved that song. Simfany danced by herself in the corner for hours. She politely turned down every chance to dance with other people down. She wanted to vibe alone. Simfany was in her zone. It seemed like all her problems went away with every sip of Hennessy she took. It felt as if her problem went away, if only that precise moment. She got lost in her bottle as she danced the night away.

***

Simfany woke up the next day with a hangover from hell. She hadn't had a hangover in years, and it was kicking her ass. She got up and made her way to the bathroom. She walked to the bathtub and turned the hot water on. She adjusted the water to the temperature she desired and let it run. As the tub filled up, Simfany took care of her hygiene. *Damn, I need to go out more, my fucking body is killing me.* She cursed herself as she poured the Epson salt into the water, hoping it would help the soreness. Simfany stepped into the hot water and relaxed. The water was soothing enough for Simfany to doze off.

A noise jarred Simfany awake. Someone was banging on her door. *Who the fuck is this? Damn!* Simfany wrapped a long beach towel around her body as she made her to the door.

"Who is it?" She called out but received no answer. "Who the fuck is knocking on my door?" she called out yet again, but still got no reply.

She walked to the door and looked out the peephole. Emilio stood on the other side of the door, talking to two of his goons. Simfany recognized them from back in the day. Simfany unlocked the door to let Emilio in.

"So, was you gone call before you came by here? Fuck wrong with you, nigga? How the fuck you know where I live anyway?" He just looked at her and said nothing, making her feel little in his world.

"Nigga, come in, but your little friends gotta go. Ain't nobody in here but me. So, they gotta leave!" Simfany said, looking in the eyes of Emilio's hired hands. Emilio looked back and nodded. Without hesitation the two left, leaving Simfany and Emilio alone.

"May I?" Emilio asked. Simfany rolled her eyes, then moved to the side to let Emilio in.

"Have a seat in the kitchen, I gotta go get dressed. Is that cool with you?" Simfany locked the front door and walked down the hall to her bedroom. *It's strange, where the fuck has Santana been?* she asked herself. She shook her head at the thoughts that had nothing to pertain to the situation at task. But regardless he was her main priority, she made a mental note to find that little nigga. *That nigga think he fucking grown.* Back to the task at hand, she got dressed. Gray sweatpants and a white T-shirt, Simfany tried to keep it as simple as possible.

She walked back into the kitchen where Emilio was occupied by a phone call. It sounded like an issue about a female. Simfany sat down and waited for the conversation to end.

"So, what do you wanna talk about, Simfany? What's been on your mind?" he asked, giving her his fully undivided attention. Simfany wasted no time in speaking what was on her mind.

"First off, why do you insist on trying to help me and my son?"

"Because I took away the nigga that would be providing for you and your son. I know you're not struggling. I hear your club is doing good numbers on the Concourse. But I'm still responsible for the heartache in ya familia."

"So, what happened that night, Emilio? What made you throw fifteen years plus of a friendship away?" she asked, tears welling in her eyes.

"How much of the truth can you handle? Because I'm gone do my best to keep it as real as possible. But before I do that, I need you to stand for me. I have to protect myself. I don't have time for any early graves or jail time. No disrespect intended, just taking precautions." Simfany stood to let Emilio search her person. Emilio started at the top of her bra strap and made his way down her body slowly. He ran his hands across the slits of her inner folds and left his hands on her ass for longer than needed. She just wanted it all to be over with. Simfany sat down and stared at Emilio with fire in her eyes.

"Satisfied? Now I want the truth, nigga!" she exclaimed.

"Damn, can a nigga get something to drink please? This shit may take a while, depending on what you all want to know." He smiled, knowing he was playing with her emotions. Without question, Simfany stood, walked to the wooden cabinet and pulled out the biggest cup she possessed. Aggravated and annoyed, she made her way to the refrigerator and

For the Love of Blood

pulled out three different kinds of Kool-Aid. She slammed them on the table. *Thud!* Emilio watched an irritated Simfany. He laughed inside. *This bitch got issues.*

"What the fuck you waiting on now? Please tell me what happened that night between you and Dracula!" Silence filled the kitchen. "Hello, nigga, anything else hindering your ability to talk. You done rubbed on my pussy, grabbed my ass, it's about time you speak or get the fuck out of my home," she softened her tone.

"Listen, let's get through this please. You know I'm gonna be upset, that's obvious. I want to know all, Emilio. Please, you owe me and Santana that much."

"First off, I don't owe you and that little nigga shit! I'm doing this to clear my mind, not yours. I told you, I'm going to tell you all that happened that night, and what happened leading up to that night. You're not going to like some parts, but you got to live with it," he replied.

"Emilio, all I want to know is why my baby was killed, because all that drunk shit not rocking with me."

"It's like this, ma." He took a deep breath and began. "Ever since you came into the picture, me and Drac hadn't seen eye to eye about a lot of things. I'm saying, we tried our best to let it pass. That nigga had known I been in love with you since our days at Lola Rodriguez. I can only speak off of my own thought, but the nigga never showed interest in you until I spoke your name. I was gone try my luck with you, so he tried his and, of course, he got what he wanted. He always got what he wanted. Yet, I still let the shit go. When you got pregnant, he continued to tell me he was about to step down and pass the torch.

"I waited patiently for my spot at the top, but of course he shitted on me again and ain't hand me shit!" He laughed at the thought. "Shit, the nigga actually took blocks away from me.

Mind you, Simfany, this a nigga I grew up with from diapers to P.A.L. I was like, damn, that fucked me up. I had to take a self-evaluation. I didn't understand why he was treating a nigga he called his brother like that. I would've killed whole blocks for that nigga! I would've laid cold for Cartez Vega. That's the nigga I know, where the loyalty we had wasn't an option.

"That nigga Dracula ... anyway, I got tired of the petty shit and started to grind on my lonely. When Dracula found out he took that shit to another level and started sending threats to mi familia. The same familia that helped raise that nigga. Me being the bigger man, I went and squashed the beef between brothers. Simfany, we were never the same. This shit is over everything the game stands for, money, power and jealousy. Fifteen years though, Simfany, fifteen fucking years ma, and that nigga treated me like I was some fucking flunkie! He wanted niggas to rely on him, fuck that. I loved that nigga, but I never been a bitch, ma.

"Anyway, the ultimate reason for his demise was because of *you.*" Emilio let his words settle in, so she could grasp at what was being said. The look on her face said it all, she felt every word that had come out of his mouth.

"Please explain," was all she could think of to say.

"The night we were rolling dice, the pot had about fifty-five hundred in it. Drac was riding with me for the pot. An old scam we use to run on the old heads when we were young niggas trying to make a way. Dracula always had issues with his pride. I said that to say this, when I bent down to collect the money *we* won, I saw you coming down the block from the store, I think. Anyway, I thought I whispered my admiration, but I guess he heard me.

"At first, he didn't know what I was talking about and who for that matter, until he turned around and saw you, after that son spazzed. I could understand at first. I was out of line, but then the son started talking greasy about how I'll never have you, so I need to stop fucking looking. I was vexed, but yet I never crossed the line. I told the nigga the only reason he pursued you was because of the shit me and him was going through. Actually, I didn't get the chance to finish the sentence, because the nigga punched me in my mouth before I could tell everybody the truth about the nigga. That's when I pulled my gun and killed him."

Simfany looked at Emilio speechless, she regained her composure and asked, "So why did you stand over him and shoot him in the head two more times?"

"Because I knew if he lived, I wouldn't. I had to kill him in order to survive. To me, it was never about the money or the power. It was about you, ma. Like I said, me and Drac had our issues before y'all started fucking around. It was a spit in my face, which was the cause of his demise. What's funny after all these years is, you never saw it. Fuck it, I'm not pressed no more."

Simfany sat silently and got her thoughts together. She wanted to be angry, but she wasn't more relieved. She finally got the story from the horse's mouth.

"So, how do you feel about me now?" she asked, surprised at her own question. Emilio sat and looked at Simfany. He thought he was hearing shit.

"What?" He had to make sure.

"You heard me. How do you feel about me now?" She moved closer up the chair.

"To be honest, like I said, you always was what I wanted, Simf. You still run through my mind on the daily. I always wanted to be with you, but I always came in last place. How you was in love with Drac all them years, that's how I was with you. I used to see you chasing son around in school and he never once acknowledged you. That we both know. He used your own crush against you. He knew though, how you think he bagged you so easily. He was confident your feelings were the same. It was a chance he was willing to take, I guess.

"What wasn't fake was the love he had when you gave him a prince to his throne. He fell in love with the thought of having a son running around. He didn't love you, ma, I don't think he did. I'm not saying that on no hating shit, you were blind to the fact though," Emilio explained.

"Do you look at me as tainted goods?" Simfany asked.

"Nah, but you don't have to try to replace what you had with Dracula with another nigga. You loved son and that's gravy." Simfany got up and sat on Emilio's lap. They looked deep into the depth of each other's eyes. She didn't know what came over her. She leaned in and kissed Emilio. At first, Emilio sat there shocked but in a second, he was kissing Simfany back. He put his tongue in her mouth, anticipating hers. Simfany suddenly stood and straddled the chair Emilio was sitting in and started kissing him again. She was truly enjoying herself. It had been so long since she was dicked down properly.

His hands roamed her body as their lips remained locked. Emilio roamed to Simfany's bra strap, and unsnapped her bra with expertise. Simfany moaned to every move Emilio made. He began to pull her shirt over her head, they stopped kissing and Simfany stood. She pulled the shirt from over her head. She admired Emilio's sexy features.

"Ma, you sure ... " Before he could finish, Simfany grabbed his hand and led him into her bedroom. Once inside the room, Simfany grabbed for Emilio's belt. She wanted to get to the erection trying to escape his pants. She felt his penis jump at every attempt to release it. Simfany pulled Emilio's pants and underwear down. She gasped. *Goddamn nigga,* she thought. Emilio was well hung.

Simfany pulled up and down on the shaft of his penis. She leaned forward and licked the tip of his penis. She looked up seductively at Emilio and their eyes met. She licked up and down his shaft and swallowed him slowly. Simfany grabbed Emilio by his ass and deep-throated his man more and more each time. She went fast, beating, sucking, licking and swirling.

Emilio was gone, he moaned through each swallow. He guided her head back and forth. Simfany looked up as she continued to suck and jack Emilio's dick.

"Shhhii... I'm bout to come, ma... I..." he moaned and shot his come down Simfany's throat. Simfany continued to jack him slowly, making sure she got every last drop. She wiped her mouth. Simfany looked up at Emilio, lost for words.

"Lay down, ma," he whispered and pushed her down onto the bed passionately. He slowly inched her sweatpants off. She lifted up her hips to help him. She wasn't wearing panties and he could smell her excitement. It was sweet to his nose. Emilio dropped to his knees and opened her legs wide. He slowly began to kiss her inner thighs, kisses became licks. Simfany moaned. He focused on her clit as he licked her up and down in circular motions. He tongue-kissed her clit as she tried to run from him. Emilio grabbed her clit in between his teeth and flicked his tongue as fast as he could.

Simfany could hold back no longer, she grabbed his head and exploded in his mouth. Emilio happily licked up the mess he made. He continued to lick around her folds while Simfany ran her fingers through his silky hair. In the process, she pushed his tongue deeper into her pussy. Her back arched from the tongue-lashing Emilio was giving her. *Damn, this nigga an expert.* He moved his tongue in and out of her as fast as he could, while he used his thumb to rub her clit in circular motions. Simfany gave a continuous moan as she humped his face. Her body began to tell on her yet again, she started to shake, she was coming again.

"Baby... I'm... mmmm... Damn... I'm... mmm," she screamed, exploding in his mouth again. Emilio slowly licked Simfany dry. Her legs trembled from the sexual bliss. Emilio wasn't done yet, he flipped Simfany over onto her stomach. He stared at the roundness of Simfany's ass.

Damn, this shorty ass so fucking fat. He stroked himself back to an erection, he played with her pussy as he hopped on to the bed. He teased her wet box with the head of his dick. He slid it up and down the wetness of her lips. Simfany could take it no more, she reached back hungrily and guided Emilio into the warmth of her walls. She moaned as the girth parted her walls. Simfany reached for a pillow and placed it between her stomach and her waist, making it to where Emilio would have all access.

Emilio stroked her to a slow pace, it drove Simfany wild as hell. When he felt like she got used to the size of his man, he grabbed Simfany by the waist and began to quicken the pace, feeding her all she could ever ask for. Simfany got into his rhythm and began throwing her ass back into him. Her ass clapped loudly around the shaft of his dick.

"Awwwwww... Fuck, fuck me, pa... Emilio... I... Awww!" her words trailed off as she moaned. She couldn't control herself. Emilio continued to dig into Simfany. She lifted onto all fours, throwing her ass back at full speed, they moved in the sync of their own music. Her legs started to shake, letting Emilio know she was about to come. He hit the bottom of her pussy, pulling her deeper into ecstasy more and more each stroke. Simfany cried out loudly as she exploded on his dick. *Damn, this nigga sex game official,* she thought

For the Love of Blood

as she rocked back and forth slowly on his dick. Emilio stiffened.

"I'm bout to come, ma, leave it or pull out?" he asked, still beating her from the back. Simfany reached behind her and took his dick into her hands. She pulled him out of her and turned around all in the same motion. She put his dick into her mouth and sucked fast, up and down, deep and shallow until he exploded.

"Damn, ma!" Simfany jerked Emilio's. dick until no more cum came out, she swallowed every last drop. Without a word spoken, Simfany got up and walked to the bathroom naked, to later return with a warm wash rag to wipe Emilio clean. She wiped herself clean as she made her way back to the bathroom.

Emilio remained in the bedroom. He was still kind of fucked up over what had just taken place. He dressed as he heard the shower turn on in the distance.

Simfany caught a glimpse of herself in the mirror. She didn't like what she saw. She saw the face of betrayal. *Fuck it,* she shrugged. *Life goes on.* She took a quick shower, combed her hair and brushed her teeth. She tried not to, but she looked into the mirror again, wondering what the fuck she had just done. She finished up and made her way back to her room. Emilio was fully dressed when she entered the room. It was an awkward silence between the two. Emilio broke the silence.

"So where does this leave us now?" he asked. Simfany sat down, half-dressed with a bath robe draped around her body. She thought about the obvious answer. She refused to respond. She just stared at him. She really didn't know what to say. Betrayal was etched all over her heart.

"You tell me, Emilio. You got what you been waiting all that time for. So, you tell me what you think should happen now," she said with tears rolling down her face.

"Whoa ma, why you crying?" Emilio asked as he got off the bed and walked toward her.

He wiped Simfany's tears away. He lifted her chin and looked into her eyes.

"You got what you wanted, no need to stick around now," she whispered and moved her face from the grasp of his hand. Emilio leaned in and embraced her.

"Ma, I'm not going nowhere. I promise, I got you from today forward. But before we go there, I need to know you forgive me for my past transgressions." He meant every word spoken. Simfany pulled out his embrace and wiped her ongoing tears.

"I got to look for Santana, I haven't seen him in two days. Thank you for the comfort. You can't be here when I come back. I promise to call you. We will work it out if we can. Just don't give up on me. This shit just got real and to be truthful, I don't think I'm ready for it," Simfany stated as she got dressed. He let her do her thing, he kissed her on the forehead and proceeded to leave the apartment. Deep down as she watched him leave, she really wanted him to stay.

That was the beginning of Simfany and Emilio, the couple did everything together, and thereafter they were inseparable. Emilio was there for her month in and month out, the bond they developed grew stronger as each day passed. Emilio helped Simfany and Santana get through the bombing of the World Trade Center on September 11, 2001. Santana had no clue Emilio was the reason he was fatherless. And of course, Simfany didn't offer the information.

The streets curled their nose at the couple but out of fear, nothing was ever spoken about it. Santana embraced Emilio the best he could. He liked Emilio for the person he was, plus he treated his mother well, that was all that mattered to him.

For the Love of Blood

Simfany looked truly happy Santana saw, but little did he know his mother was sleeping with the enemy. Literally.

Emilio got comfortable with the now. He loved Simfany so much he went against the street code and gave her the combinations and codes to where his money was kept. Even though he knew she would never do anything out the way, it was still a no-no in the game we call the streets. His intentions were to give her the access for a case of an emergency. He loved Simfany dearly, so he gave her the benefit of the doubt. He never doubted her loyalty, and vice versa.

***

Simfany called Emilio, wanting to know why he blew her off for the date they had planned.

"What's up, ma?" he answered, recognizing Simfany's number.

"Where the fuck you at, nigga? So, you blowing me off now?" she asked angrily.

"Damn ma, I apologize. I'm in Harlem right now. Something came up that needed to be handled."

"Where are you though?"

"In Harlem with my Rasta niggas on 143rd and Amsterdam." Telling her in code he was with his connect handling business.

"When you coming home?" she sounded concerned.

"Where you at now?" he asked.

"In ya spot, waiting for some of that daddy dick. I been waiting for a while too," she said seductively.

"Aight, I'll be there in thirty minutes. Don't leave, I promise to make it up to you. Again ma, I apologize."

"You're forgiven, papi, but it bet not happen again. I'll see you when you get here. I love you, Emilio," she replied into the phone.

"You know I love you too, ma." He hung up and continued his business at hand. Emilio's apartment was located in the heart of the hood, the 700 building of Melrose Houses. The building was located in the center of Melrose. It wasn't where he laid his head, it was a spot to chill and look over his investment. Nobody knew about that particular apartment. With Simfany in his ear, he decided to set up shop in his old stomping ground. Only this time, he played his position from behind the scenes. Plus, he looked at it a certain way being a player in the game of life. He realized no matter who you are or how much fear you instill, the streets play for keeps. Sides are never open for debate. Whoever has what it takes to claim the throne, all spots are up for grabs.

"I'm on top of my fucking game," he said to himself as he sped down the highway. with eight neatly wrapped bricks of cocaine in the trunk of his car. What made it more interesting was the thought of the beautiful woman he had waiting on him at home. Nothing could go wrong in his world.

He arrived back home twenty or so minutes earlier than expected, grabbed the duffle bag out the trunk and made his way to his apartment building. As he approached, he noticed that the lights were off in his apartment. *Damn, she better not have left,* he thought as he made his way into the building. Emilio made his way upstairs, bag in hand, with his other hand on his ratchet just for precaution. He finally made it upstairs and put the key into the door and stepped in.

"Simfany!" he called out.

"Simfany, ma, you still here?" he called out again, raising his voice louder.

For the Love of Blood

"I'm in the back, papi, come get this sweet pussy," she yelled from the back. Emilio smiled as he walked to the kitchen and placed the duffle bag on the kitchen counter. He walked to the back, peeling off articles of clothing. *Damn, this bitch always on some freaky shit.*

He smiled to himself, down for whatever. He got to the doorframe of his room and opened the door. He tried to adjust his eyes to the darkness of the room. Simfany said nothing, but Emilio could see her approaching seductively.

"Come give daddy some love, ma, I've missed you all day." He bit his lip as she continued to move closer. What he didn't see was the Glock 26 she had concealed behind her back. Before Emilio could speak another word, she raised the gun and squeezed the trigger.

Boc...Boc...Boc...Boc... Hitting Emilio in his torso and neck area, he fell back from the impact of the shells.

"Aaaaaaarrrgggghhhhhh ma, what the fuck?" he screamed as blood poured out of his wounds. He slowly slid down the wall into a sitting position. He looked up at death in the eye of the barrel. Simfany walked over to Emilio and stood over him.

"Loyalty is everything, papi. See you in hell, puta!" she said as she raised the gun.

Boc ... Boc... Boc... Boc... Boc... Boc... Boc... squeezing until the magazine emptied and the Glock stopped busting, indicating the clip was empty.

"Now you can rest in peace, my love. I'm sorry it took what it took to do this, but always know my love has never faded. Te amo papi, siempre," she said, talking to Dracula's memory, hoping he could hear her and understand. Simfany grabbed the bag she had sitting at the base of the bedroom door. She walked to the door, only seconds from leaving, but the black duffle bag that sat alone on the kitchen counter caught her attention. She quickly grabbed it and left the apartment. Simfany made it back home and checked the bag's content. One bag contained an undisclosed amount of money and guns. When she opened the duffle bag she picked off the counter, eight neatly wrapped duffle bags looked back at her.

The sound of keys made Simfany jump from paranoia. She was nervous. She hurried and put the two duffle bags into her closet. She popped a new clip into her Glock. She crept to the bedroom door and watched as the apartment door. The door opened and she raised her gun to eye level, hidden in the darkness of the house. Santana and Justice walked in, closing the door behind them. Simfany lowered the Glock.

Her heart rate was at an unreasonable pace. Simfany had to lie down. Unwanted sleep took hold of her. She slept the best she ever slept in a long while, she didn't know if it was because of the death of Emilio or the comfort the Glock gave her. She fell asleep, gun in hand, forming a habit that would last forever.

Simfany had no real intention of going hard with Emilio; it was a plot that needed to be done to get back at the person that took her baby daddy away from her and Santana. Simfany saw the opportunity, so she took it. Despite what Emilio said that night about Dracula, she knew the truth. She knew Drac loved her, she knew what needed to be done, so she did just that.

The little things Emilio did for her and Santana, she felt Drac was supposed to be doing. That angered her most, which helped take the fear out of her and kill Emilio. She fucked the nigga for months and it finally paid off, literally. In more ways than one. *Karma is a bitch. Cartez, you can handle that nigga now,* she thought many times after the murder.

***

The streets were hungry for blood, after Emilio's body was found in his home. Even though he was envied more than he was loved, he was still respected by the people who really mattered. There was an eyewitness that said they saw a female leaving the apartment after the shots were fired, but no one knew who the female was or what she even looked like. Even though Emilio's soldiers checked on Simfany often, Simfany's paranoia got the best of her. She was paranoid everywhere she went.

She finally made the decision to leave New York behind and start fresh, she had all the money she needed to do so. Simfany had a friend in Maryland she grew up with back in high school. She thought it would be a good idea to visit and see what Baltimore had to offer. Simfany wanted to wait until the right time to tell Santana, she knew it wouldn't go well. He was the definition of a true New Yorker. He was going to be hurt the most to leave his life in the city.

Winter 2001

School was out for the Christmas break, and Simfany had the idea of moving on her mind again. She let the last thought be just that, a thought. But now she wanted to act on it. She was tired of the bullshit. She needed to talk to Santana about the move she wanted to make. No matter what his opinions were, they were still leaving, but she still owed him the respect to let him know in advance. It was a blow, but it had to be done.

"Santana, where are you? Come help me with these damn groceries," she yelled as she came through the door with bags in her hands.

"Here I come," he yelled from the back room. Santana walked from his room to the kitchen.

"What's up, beautiful?" He walked over to his mother and kissed her on her cheek, grabbing the bags out of her hands. Simfany smiled. She knew he would understand, for her sake she hoped so.

"Tana, we have to talk."

"About what?" he asked, still putting food away.

"I want to leave New York."

"What! Why?" He stopped, giving his mother his undivided attention.

"Too much shit has been happening around here and it's starting to become too much. I want to raise my son, not bury him."

"That still don't explain nothing, you grew up in these streets and you know what it is. My father was killed in cold blood and yet you never moved. There has to be more to it. So, tell me why." He looked at his mother with a smug look.

"Santana, we're leaving New York." He didn't respond. "Santana!"

"Why, because a nigga killed your boyfriend?" before she could answer he continued ... "I wanna stay, you can go." The comment hurt Simfany to the bottom of her soul. She couldn't believe what just came out of his mouth. They were a team, had been for the last twelve years. The words truly cut deep. Anger overcame her.

"Nigga, you not staying here, point fucking blank!" she blinked back tears. His tone changed and his face grew flush. Santana could see the hurt on his mother's face.

"Look Ma, can I at least finish the school year? You might change your mind. Justice and Auntie would love for me to

For the Love of Blood

stay with them until then. Please, Ma. Think about this." Santana walked over to his mother and wiped the running tears away.

"You know I love you, Ma, more than I love myself or anything else in this world. I didn't mean to make you cry. All I'm asking is to give thought to this. I do want to stay for the rest of the school year," he pleaded.

"If Lonnie say you can stay until June, it's good with me. But Santana, I swear after the school year, we as a team are leaving. You hear me?" She buckled to the charm of her son like she always did. "You sure you don't want to come to Maryland with me? You can help me find a good spot to live."

"I'll be down in June, and if you're serious about the move then I guess that's gone be our new spot. Hopefully, you change your mind though." He smiled, wanting to lighten up the mood. Santana hugged his mother. "I love you, pretty lady." He pecked a kiss on the side of her face.

"Siempre." Simfany smiled. Santana went back to his room, leaving Simfany with the groceries and her thoughts.

***

Simfany packed up later than expected, leaving Santana with Justice and Lonnie. Simfany went to Baltimore and got herself situated, moving to the infamous Edmondson Avenue on the city's west side. Only if she knew that moving to Baltimore would change her and Santana's life forever, she would've never left New York. Being three months away from Santana's birthday, he was ecstatic about seeing his mother. The upcoming summer was predicted to be the hottest one yet, and shit had the potential of getting real with each day that passed. This summer was the beginning of what made a G...

Chapter 3

"My nigga Edwin just got shot!" Justice yelled through the phone.

"Calm down, son, where you at?" Santana asked.

"In the big park, son laid out bleeding from his face. Tana, he not moving, son! I think he gone... I think my nigga..." Justice cried, fearing the worst. His cousin might be dead.

"My nigga he not dead, don't think like that," Santana said, trying to calm his best friend down, even though he didn't believe his own words. Edwin and his family moved into the hood from Mott Haven Projects. They weren't from Courtlandt, but had family ties, so they were loved just the same.

"Where Day Day and Quan at? Santana asked, thinking of Edwin's younger brothers.

"Everybody ran when the shots rang out."

"Then how you know Big E got hit?"

"We were running side by side and he dropped. I couldn't just leave him. I ducked my head and held his." Justice was frantic. The streets had been a war zone since Emilio's death. Emilio's young bulls from Philly wanted blood. They came for answers but were given the runaround, but that was only because nobody knew anything. So, they took action leaving one dead and three badly wounded.

"C.A.N. out here trippin' right now son. I think they killed the nigga Ill Will. Those Philly niggas got shit out here crazy right now," Justice explained to Santana, referring to the Courtlandt Avenue Niggas.

"Here I come, I'll be there in a second. Stay the fuck out the way, son. I'm coming, you hear me?" Santana got dressed as fast as possible and made his way outside. Everyone was outside and there were crowds of people everywhere. The biggest was in the big park. The Big Park is located in the center of Melrose Houses. Santana jogged to the crowd. He saw ambulance lights as he approached the scene. Edwin was being put into the ambulance, a good sign, he figured. Big E was about three or four years older than them. He was well liked because he was one of the older niggas who had love for the youngins. He was also Va-Holla, second-in-command to Bogus.

Santana searched the crowd for his best friends, Justice and Peewee. Peewee was nowhere in sight, he continued to look and found Justice holding Missy, Edwin's little sister. Calling her beautiful was an understatement. The Dominican blood that ran through her veins showed. He approached them, still no sign of Day Day and Quan.

"You aight, ma?" Santana asked Missy. She nodded her head. She pulled her face away from Justice's chest.

"Yeah, I'm okay," Missy replied. Santana hugged her and kissed her on her forehead.

"Keep ya head up, beautiful, big bro will pull through."

"Thank you, Santana, I hope so." She bowed her head back to Justin's chest and continued to cry.

For the rest of the night, the rest of the hood stayed on point. Kids were kept in the house. Edwin didn't die, but he did take a bullet to his face, leaving him in a coma. Will was shot three times in the back, leaving him paralyzed from the waist down. A mother and her child were also shot; the mother, killed. Santana was definitely going to take his mother up on her offer of moving to Baltimore. Shit was getting crazy in the hood. Bullets were hitting anything moving. A change of scenery was due. The only thing he hated was to leave Justice and Peewee behind. No matter how he felt, he knew he had no choice in the matter.

For the Love of Blood

***

It was August 7, Santana's thirteenth birthday. He sat alone at his father's gravesite. It was his first year away from his mother. He missed both his parents. Santana looked at the tombstone and shed silent tears with eager thoughts of, what if.

"I love you, Pa. I wish you could have been here for us. I still don't understand everything, but eventually I will. It's not a day that goes by that I don't think about you. I promise to take care of *our* pretty lady." He wiped his tears and laid the picture of him and his mother against the tombstone.

***

Simfany heard about the shooting that took place in Melrose, she was worried about Santana. The school year was already over, but she decided to let Santana stay for the rest of the summer. After hearing the news of the four people that got shot, she had no plan of leaving him in New York no longer. It was also Santana's birthday, and she felt his absence. It was also her first year ever away from her son on his birthday. She called his number from memory.

"What's up, pretty lady?" Santana answered, recognizing his mother's number.

"I hear it's been crazy out there, when was you gone call and tell me?" she asked angrily.

"That's why when I talked to you last night, I didn't tell you. I knew you were going to start trippin'. I was in the house with Lonnie when that shit happened. Flocko and the twins got shit back in order out here."

"Yeah, whatever. I'm coming to get you this weekend, so have your shit packed and ready to go. Anyway, happy birthday, baby. Sorry I'm not— "

"No need to explain, Ma, I know if you could, you would be here. I went and saw Daddy today." The phone went silent.

"I love you, Santana. Always know that, okay? Be safe please." He understood why she wanted to avoid that conversation. He respected it and dropped the subject.

"Ight, Ma, I'll be ready, and you know I love you. See you this weekend. Oh, and thank you for the birthday money you sent me. I'm not mad at you and I will never be mad at you, please understand that. What's understood is enough for me. Stop stressing, I'm good." That put a smile on Simfany's face.

"Okay, I love you, boy."

"Love you too, Ma."

***

The day came for Santana to say his goodbyes. He first made his way to the projects across the street, Jackson Houses Marissa was the first person he needed to see. As Santana crossed the street, he spotted Summer standing in front of building 301, crying her eyes out. He thought it was from another nigga breaking her beautiful heart, but little did he know his presence was missed before he even left.

"What's up, ma, you alright?" he asked as he hugged her. She didn't respond, she just continued to cry. She cried silently on his shoulder for what seemed like a lifetime. It always hurt Santana to see a female in a fucked-up state. He had nothing to say, because he had other things on his mind, Marissa. Summer pulled away and wiped her face. She pulled him into her and kissed him on his lips, she then backed away.

For the Love of Blood

"I will always love you, Santana, don't be a stranger, baby," she said as she walked away with new tears forming in her eyes. Santana could tell his leaving hurt Summer to the core. She was his heart, but only in a different light than she saw him. Summer was like a big sister, she just wanted more than he was willing to give her. He always promised himself he would never cross that line. Not now, not never. Santana turned and walked into the building. He boarded the elevator and pressed the ninth floor. Santana thought of the best words to say as he made his way down the hall to Marissa's apartment. He came up blank. He stood in front of the door, took a deep breath, and then knocked.

The peep hole light went dark, indicating that someone was looking out the other end of the door. Seconds later, the door opened. There stood the love of his life, Marissa Nunez, with tears also running down her face. She looked bad, it pulled at Santana's heart strings, but at the end of the day, it was nothing he could fix how she felt.

"Come in." Marissa said in a low whisper, she then moved to the side.

"You aight ma?" Santana walked into the apartment. Marissa locked the door and followed Santana into the living room. They both sat down, each facing one another.

"I'm gone miss you, ma, but like I've told you before, if I could stay, I would. You know my mom's not letting that rock, especially after that big shootout in Melrose last week. Shit, I'm surprised she let me stay this long for real." What he said didn't seem to help none.

"Listen, Santana, just always know you'll always have my heart. No matter who I'm with, you will always be my baby. I swear to God, please don't..." she began to cry again. "Santana, please don't leave me!" she begged. He knew coming to see her would be difficult. He embraced Marissa to show some type of comfort. He ran his fingers through her hair as she laid on his chest.

"I'm gone come back for you, ma. You hear me?" he tried to reassure her. Marissa looked up.

"Promise me then."

"You know how I feel about promises, ma, promises are meant to be broken. But I will try my best, is that good enough for right now?" He still didn't know if it was the truth or not. He didn't know what the future held. He motioned for her to get up, as he stood.

"Where you going?" she asked confusingly.

"I got to say goodbye to my niggas, ma, I'll be back if I still got time before I leave. My mother is on the road now. I don't have much time," he explained.

"Please keep in touch and stay away from these Baltimore bitches. I mean it, Santana. I love you, baby." She wrapped her arms around his neck and kissed him deeply. It would be the last time he would ever kiss her. They both knew that.

"I love you too, Marissa." Santana left without saying another word. He didn't want to turn around because of the tears now running down his face. He didn't want to show that kind of emotion. He made it inside the elevator and cried. He felt like he was losing a big part of his heart, leaving Marissa behind. He held his head up and wiped his eyes.

Santana exited the building, roamed around and said goodbye to all the people that mattered to him. He walked to the crowd of boys chilling on the basketball court.

"I hear you out today for sure curly fries," Nalevi said.

"Yeah, my mom's moved to Baltimore, so I have no choice. That shit whack, but you know, family first."

"Damn, we gone miss you with your short ass." They all laughed.

"I know I'm gone miss my Ave niggas too. But look, my G, y'all niggas be safe and bring that championship home for me." He slapped his team mates up, DJ, Pop, Ounnie, Clue, Josh, Psycho D and Nalevi. Those were the niggas that taught him the love of the game.

"I'm gone miss y'all niggas, son."

"Be safe, curly fries," they all said simultaneously, Santana nodded and walked on his way. Justice and Peewee were waiting in front of 304, shooting a basketball into a blue trash can.

"Be safe out there, son, you know the hood gone miss ya pretty boy ass. Don't become one of those niggas, aight? This where you're from. Florida changed John John," Peewee said. He shot the ball into the trash can making the basket

"That's the last thing you have to worry about, I'll never forget where I'm from, my nigga. That's on hood," Santana replied with an ounce of pride.

"Is all your stuff packed and ready to go?" Justice asked like a caring parent.

"Nah, I'm bout to go do that now."

"Nigga, you trippin', you know Simfany ain't playing. Come on, son." They dapped Peewee up and made their way up to Justice's apartment to finish packing.

Simfany arrived at around 3:30 later that day. She helped Santana carry his bags to the car as he said goodbye to all his friends that waited for him on the curb. After she said her hellos and her goodbyes to some people, they hit the road back home to Body More, Murda Land. They arrived back in Baltimore before the sun dropped Simfany stayed over west on Edmonson and Carey.

Santana would soon learn about this second city he would call home, but it was a city he refused to adapt to. Simfany gave Santana a tour of the house. After Santana got settled in, she left with the promise to return soon. As soon as he finished unpacking his clothes in his new room, he called Justice to let him know he was good.

"Yo," Justice answered the phone.

"I'm here, son, this shit looks dirtier than the Yitty. The townhouse my mom got is hot though. But how you holding and what you got planned tonight?"

"Shit, I'm good, fam, bout to go to The Key with Peewee. They got this pajama contest tonight, the winner get like three bills. I need that. You be safe down there, man, you're missed already, and it hasn't even been twenty-four hours. But look, my nigga, I'm about to go over to Jackson's real quick. I love you, my nigga, no homo." They both laughed at Justice's last comment.

"I love you too, son, I'm out. Tell everybody I send my love."

"Aight, one." Justice hung up. Santana was homesick already. He missed his city and his friends. He put the phone back into its cradle. Santana heard Simfany's key trying to fit into the lock, so he walked over and opened the door for her. She came in, carrying groceries from a store called Food Lion. Once Simfany got the bags settled and put away, she handed him a flier of some sort. He read it, then looked up at her.

"What's this?" he asked.

"It's a flier for the Stone Soul Picnic," she replied.

"And that's what exactly?" he asked, being a smart ass.

"They have live performances and shit like that. They serve food. Umm, it's like Pelham Bay Park on the Fourth, just with performers. I heard it was nice. I want you to come with me, pleeeease. Will you? Your birthday just passed, and I want to give you more than money can buy. Happiness with me." She laughed at her corniness. "So, what's up, you going

For the Love of Blood

to go with an old lady like me?" she asked Santana with his own signature puppy dog eyes.

"If you want me to, then I got you. It can't be that bad," he replied. Simfany smiled. Santana had no real worries going to the picnic he just hoped it wasn't true about Baltimore niggas hating New York niggas. He brought something with him, so at the end of the day, it didn't really matter how anyone felt. After Edwin got shot in the hood, he, Justice and Peewee went and bought guns for protection. Well actually, Bogus gave them the guns for the free look. Santana got a .380 Jennings, Justice and Peewee picked matching 9-millimeter handguns. He wasn't the best when it came to firing, but he knew enough when he needed to ring that bitch. He and Peewee used to go under P.S. 151 to practice shooting their guns. So, he was kind of gun savvy.

Santana walked up the stairs to his new room and pulled the gun from his shoebox and looked over the chrome plating. A smile fell across his face as he pointed the gun in the mirror at himself. He felt like God in a sense, with the cold metal resting in his hands. He knew what he had in his grip, life and death. *If Bogus could just see me now,* he thought.

He snapped back to sanity when he heard Simfany's movement downstairs. He hurried and put the gun away. That's the last thing he wanted her to know he had in her house. Santana organized his room to his liking. After he was finished putting everything away, he crawled into his new comfortable bed and finally drifted off.

It was a beautiful day in Baltimore City, especially for a picnic to take place. The radio stations had been talking about the events that would take place at the picnic. Simfany was excited when she and Santana arrived at Druid Hill Park around noon. When they arrived, it was surprisingly drama free of the antics that was rumored to take place each year. But then again, she had to think it was still early. Yet Simfany still had a positive vibe by the people already present.

The live performances were a plus and she was definitely looking forward to that. It would be close to five hundred or more people in attendance before sundown.

On the other hand, Santana wasn't feeling the atmosphere, not because it was boring, but because he didn't know anybody. He was uncomfortable. He knew he was an outsider, and he knew what happened to outsiders. He knew how they got down in his borough, better yet, his hood. You weren't sliding through if you weren't welcomed, so at the end of the day he knew what it was with these Baltimore niggas, or at least he thought he did. No matter what, Santana was prepared for whatever, he was heavily strapped up. But he prayed he wouldn't have to use it.

Despite his uneasiness, he began to have fun and enjoy the music. The females paraded around with little to nothing on. Santana was young but grabbed the attention of females of all ages. His mother was nowhere to be found, and that was cool with him. He didn't want to ruin her day by being stubborn. Santana's thoughts drifted him through the park on a sight-see.

He walked until he came upon a lake. He looked in disgust at the water, it was dirty as hell. He wondered how many souls laid at the bottom of that lakebed. Baltimore was known for its climbing murder rate. Bored, Santana walked back to the festival. As he made his way back, he saw a commotion taking place. His attention reverted to the crowd. Being nosey, he walked into the midst of the onlookers and noticed two females fighting. He couldn't really see much because of the people surrounding them. Santana searched the crowd for his mother to make sure she was okay.

She should be around here somewhere. I know she can see this crowd forming, he thought as he continued to search for her through the sea of faces. As he made his way through the crowd and got closer to the fight, his heart stopped. Simfany was one of the women fighting. Proudly, she was on top doing her thing. Instinctively, Santana ran over, trying to break up the fight. His small frame couldn't manage no matter how hard he tried to pull them apart. Santana looked back, hoping someone would help, but no one came. Eventually, people did come from the crowd to help give assistance, separating the females from each other. Santana pulled on Simfany's arm. She wouldn't budge. He looked at her face, which was marked with small scratches. Santana instantly got enraged from the look of his mother's face.

"Ma!" he yelled, trying to get her attention. She looked at him. "You alright? What happened?" he asked.

"Fuck that bitch, that's why I beat that ass, bitch!" she screamed at the girl still being helped off the ground.

"Ya face scratched and bleeding, Ma, let's go." Simfany went to protest, but he pulled her arm forcefully. She stopped resisting and followed behind him. Out of the corner of his eye, he saw a fist coming at his mother. She saw it also, but it was too late to react. It came fast, way too fast to dodge. The punch connected, dropping Simfany to the grass. Her body collapsed from the force of the hit. The only thing Santana could do was stop her from falling on her face.

He laid his mother down gently. What had just happened angered him to no end. His mother was laying in the grass as a man stood over her and talked shit. He couldn't even understand what the guy was saying because he was so mad. All he saw was red.

He cradled his mother's head in his arms. A tear rolled down his face as he looked into Simfany's face. This was a moment that his father was supposed to be there to protect them both. Santana pulled his mother's face into his chest and mugged the crowd as it formed around them. Simfany stirred. As she slowly began to regain consciousness, she instantly began to cry from the pressure of the hit. It broke Santana's heart to see his mother like that. The dude that hit her was still talking shit as Santana helped her up. Once Simfany was on her feet, he turned to dude and let him know what was on his mind.

"Fuck you, you bitch ass nigga. You hit a female. Nigga, you think you tough? You a bitch, son." Santana only stood at about five feet and some change but was ready to bang over his moms. He had the soul of a lion, a trait he inherited not only from his mother, but his father also.

"That's what's wrong with you out of town muthafuckas, thinking y'all untouchable. Nigga, you better stay in a child's place."

"Fuck you, bitch!" Santana was ready for war. The girl Simfany had beaten minutes before was trying to pull dude away from the scene, but he refused to leave.

"Jimdog, come on nigga, the police will be here soon. Fuck that bitch," she pleaded as her Baltimore accent peaked, she pronounced Jimdog as Jim Doug. He still wouldn't budge.

"Nah, shorty your youngin' out here thinking he tough, I see. You better calm the fuck down before I knock you out too!" Jimdog warned. Jimdog advanced toward Simfany again as if he was about to hit her yet again.

"Nigga, you got me fucked up," was all Santana said as he raised his .380 handgun.

"What the fuck is that going to do? You gone bust over this bitch?" Before Jimdog could laugh at his humorless comment, Santana pulled the trigger. *Boc... Boc... Boc...* hitting Jimdog in his stomach, dropping him to the ground.

For the Love of Blood

"Pussy nigga!" Santana spat on him. The crowd scattered at the sound of the gunfire. He stood there dazed with a hit gun in his hand. Simfany cried out, she knew she might have lost her son forever. Santana stood over Jimdog as he tried to crawl away. Simfany tried to stop him and pull him away from Jimdog's body on the ground. Santana couldn't move. He just stared at Jimdog as he made feeble attempts to get away. Blood poured out of his body at a rapid pace.

Santana raised his gun again to fire, but Simfany grabbed his hand before he got the chance to pull the trigger. Santana snapped out of his momentary daze when he heard the approaching police sirens. He and Simfany walked in the opposite direction of the oncoming sirens. He turned and looked at his mother,

"Are you okay, pretty lady?" She nodded, still shocked at what had just taken place. Tears stained her face. Even though the impact from the blow didn't leave much damage, her face was still swollen. "I love you, Ma, I'll never let another nigga put his hands on you. I'm sorry it even went that far." They continued to walk.

"It's not your fault what he did to me. I love you for protecting me. Don't ever be sorry you saved Mommy's life." She stopped and embraced him. It was an emotional moment, but quickly passed because of the severity of the situation. They were almost near the lake when they both heard the shout.

"Freeze!" the police officer yelled with his gun drawn. Santana looked up at Simfany.

She stood in front of Santana to protect him from the barrel of the gun. When the officer made his way closer to the pair, Simfany turned around and whispered to Santana, "Run, baby."

He didn't wait for another word, he took off. The Baltimore police officer took off after him. Santana ran past the lake and threw the gun in the water. He hit West 29th Street. He frantically ran until he didn't see anyone behind him. He cut in and out of alleys, awaiting patrol cars, but none came or flew by. He ran off 29th and hit North Charles Street. He looked around again, of course he didn't recognize anything nearby. He was no longer running, he slowed down to a steady walk. Santana continued to walk up North Charles Street, until he stopped by a sign that read *Loyola University of Maryland*. A car behind him screeched to a halt, he looked back and again it was the Baltimore Police Department on his ass, guns drawn, only this time they looked like they were ready to fire.

"I dare you to run this time, you lor bastard," the officer from the park said. Santana put his hands up and surrendered. One of the officer's holstered his gun, walked over and placed Santana in handcuffs.

"You have the right to remain silent, you have the right…" Santana's mind drifted off as he was put into the back seat of the awaiting police car. As he sat in the back of the car, he knew his life would forever change.

Santana was taken down to the precinct and booked for attempted murder and felonious assault. After his booking was complete, he was sent to the Charles H. Hickey School for Boys.

After he arrived at the Hickey School, he showered and was allowed his free phone call to his immediate family. Santana called his mother.

"Hello!" Simfany picked up after the second ring with urgency in her tone.

"Ma, they booked me for attempted murder and felonious assault. I'm at some place called the Hickey School, it's in Baltimore County," he explained what he was told by the officer that transported him.

"Are you okay? I love you, baby. I'll be there at your first court date they set. You hear me? I'm going to get the directions and I'll be up there as soon as possible. Tana, I love you, baby boy." He heard her start to sob through the phone. He tried to bring reassurance.

"I'm good, how is your face feeling?"

"Still swollen, but it'll get better with time. Please remember Mommy loves you dearly, Santana." She couldn't stop the tears from flowing.

"Stop crying, Ma, this isn't your fault. I don't care what you said or did, that nigga shouldn't have put his hands on you. I will protect you till my dying day. Never forget that. I'll be okay though, please don't worry too much about me, you raised a G."

"I'm so sorry for this, baby."

"Chill with all the apologies, I'm for real. My time is up, Ma, I love you. I'll call back whenever I can."

"Love you, and please stay out of trouble if you can, don't let these people make you out to be a monster."

"Alright, pretty lady, I got you. You just make sure you keep your head held high," Santana replied. Simfany ended the phone call. Her baby was locked up at the age of thirteen, facing adult time because of her actions. Simfany sat back against the bedpost and thought back to all the bullshit that took place, leading up to Santana going to jail.

Jamel Mitchell

Chapter 4

Spring 2002

Simfany brought the drama with her from New York, her duffle bag. The cocaine, the money and guns were enough to get people killed, a war started, and her son, damn near a life sentence. Simfany needed the coke moved, so she set out to find a source to do just that. On a night out, Simfany met a Puerto Rican nigga named Byrd that lived over East Baltimore, Jefferson and Rose. He was a Latrobe Project veteran. He was well respected in East Baltimore. He was a henchman for the infamous Carlos Rivera.

Carlos supplied both East and West Baltimore, he dipped and dabbled in the North and South drug trade. He also had a hold on the surrounding counties. Simfany's friend, Carol, introduced her to Byrd at club *Hammer Jacks*. Simfany and Byrd hit it off the first time they met. Their friendship turned into a loyalty they could understand. He trusted Simfany in the little time they knew each other. Whether she wanted to or not, she trusted him also. Byrd told Simfany everything about himself and some of his past, not all is privy to certain people he believed. He believed her enough though, more than anyone else.

Little did Byrd know she was sitting in his demise, she needed eight bricks flipped, and she needed Byrd. After a while, she no longer had intentions on using Byrd to move the cocaine. But she knew he had the sources and she needed it to be gone soon. Simfany didn't like the fact of having so much coke in her home.

The memories sent chills through her body as she sat on her bed and thought about the fatal conversation that started the biggest war that the city of Baltimore would ever see.

"Byrd, where you at?" she called out from the kitchen of her town.

"I'm in the living room, shorty!" he called back. She made her way into the living room.

Byrd was playing the game when Simfany walked in. He acknowledged her but was engulfed in the television screen.

"What's up, shorty?"

"I got a surprise for you, pa. I need you to do something for me." She gave him her playful puppy eyes and poked her lips out. He frowned, but he had to admit, *Simfany is so beautiful.*

"You know I don't like surprises, dog." Byrd was suddenly on point.

"My name is not Doug," she said playfully, making fun of his accent.

"I know, baby, but you'll like this," Simfany said. She got up from her seat and went upstairs. He thought hard. *What the fuck kind of shit she got? A surprise for me?* He heard her in the master bedroom. Byrd got up and retrieved his Glock 17. He checked the clip and it was fully loaded. He knew how bitches got down, he used them himself to execute niggas. He would be ready for whatever if Simfany was on some bullshit. Byrd sat back on the cream-colored sofa and waited. He waited for Simfany and her *surprise*, with his Glock resting on his lap. He watched as Simfany came back downstairs, carrying a duffle bag. She sat the bag on the glass table in front of him.

"Open it up," she told him.

"You open it," he replied, being aware of the possibility of betrayal.

"Nigga, what the fuck wrong with you?" she asked, suddenly noticing his demeanor. He was tense.

"What are you talking about?" He tried to play dumb.

"Nigga, you may not have taught me all the tricks of the trade, but you taught me enough. I can see you're real tense right now, but why?" She was confused. Byrd pulled the Glock off his lap, he went against his better judgment and sat it on the table.

"You know how these breezy's are, shorty, I don't know what to expect. Not even from my own mother. My apologies, I meant no disrespect. What you got for me?" He tried to change the subject to make it less awkward. He sat up close enough to get to his gun if he needed to. His murderous instinct took over in the simplest situations. He grabbed the black bag and opened it. Byrd had to double look at the contents in the bag. He looked up. He could still see the disappointment on Simfany's face as she lightly smiled.

"Where you get this shit from, shorty?" he asked, puzzled.

"Not important, do you know anybody that can move it for me?" He looked into Simfany's eyes to see if she was serious or not. The look on her face was enough to assure him the severity of her comment.

"I can move it." He looked in the bag again. "How many here shorty?" he asked.

"Eight."

"How much you want back?"

"A hundred and sixty thou. That's at twenty a brick. I know what they can go for, so I dropped the price. So, will you help?"

"I got you, Simf, but there's only one problem with that."

"And that is what?"

"Carlos." The name told its own story. He owned Baltimore's drug trade. He would kill both Byrd and Simfany if he found out.

"Man, fuck," she cursed, forgetting about the reign Carlos had over Baltimore.

"But we may be able to get around that though. I got a couple of young niggas in the county who getting brick money. Hopefully, I can feed them, and they can feed us."

"What county, you talking about them niggas in Dundalk? Those Dundalk niggas too hot."

"Nah the youngins I speak of are from Harford County. He and his blood homies got Edgewood on lock," he explained, thinking of Hood Ru and his Tree Top Piru familia.

"If you think they got what it takes, then I'm down," she replied.

Byrd called Hood Ru and they talked business. They made the necessary plans to meet and talk prices. The meeting went well, and he sold the cocaine at twenty-six a brick. Hood bought two bricks and was given two on consignment. Hood knew who he was, so Byrd wasn't worried about Hood acting up when it came to his money. The coke was gone within a week and a half. That left Byrd with fifty-six bands to maneuver with. Simfany was elated when Byrd hit her with her money. Byrd explained to her his view on copping more weight, but Simfany was against it. She only wanted to get rid of the eight she had from killing Emilio.

Eventually, Byrd became the counties' steady connect. He was big in Edgewood and its surrounding counties. His name rang bells in Aberdeen, Havre de Grace, and even Abingdon.

Simfany watched Byrd slowly climb to the top. Byrd was well respected and feared in the streets, so his reputation preceded him well. Hood Ru and his blood homies bought brick after brick from Byrd, but Byrd didn't seem to realize, he was fucking with Carlos's money. Tree Top Piru is one of the most known street gangs in West Baltimore's 3rd Ward neighborhood, Edmonson and beyond to the East. Hood was brought under the five by a man named Tech. Tech dealt with Carlos before he was incarcerated years earlier. Carlos gave the gang

For the Love of Blood

protection, if needed, from the gang unit and the lurking stick-up boys. They had no worries of any kind, not that it mattered with a team of killers. It was business. Byrd had the bricks for the low and the rest just seemed to fall into place. But when Tech got locked up, Hood was put in the forefront to run the business. Business was swell on the part of Hood and his team, but the moves weren't sitting well with Carlos. He heard of the moves Hood was making behind his back.

At first, he couldn't believe the betrayal. Carlos approached the situation like a true boss, he contacted Hood Ru and told him what was being said through the streets and told him if it was true, it needed to stop. Hood was to deal with him and him only. Carlos made himself clear. Hood heard what he was saying, but he couldn't care less how the old man felt. Carlos' demands fell on deaf ears. Only a few knew who Carlos was and what he was capable of, and Hood wasn't one of them. Carlos felt a message needed to be sent, but out of respect for Tech he played fair. Business got back to its usual, but once again Hood's loyalty was in question.

This time, Carlos found out Byrd was the mysterious connect supplying the clique full of young niggas. Shit, Byrd was actually supplying the whole county. That threw Carlos for a loop; he wasn't ready for that kind of knowledge. Byrd was his main soldier, and the only person he trusted in Baltimore City. The deceit played tricks in his mind, so he devised a plan. His father always told him you know niggas real intentions when money is involved. Carlos had a plan to test Byrd's.

He was going to put a hit out on Hood Ru and any of his soldiers. Hood was who Carlos really wanted, so the bounty was higher. Carlos called Byrd and explained to him the reason for the hit, how much it paid, and where to locate his target. Byrd took the hit and proceeded to do his homework to fulfill the contract. Byrd backed out when he realized who he was being paid to kill. Byrd called Carlos.

"Aye, poppa. How you doing?" Carlos answered.

"I need to talk to you, it's important," Byrd replied.

"Food court, White Marsh, papi." Carlos hung the phone up.

The time came for Byrd and Carlos to sit down. It was a beautiful spring day outside, as they met in the food court on the top floor of the mall. The place was one of their normal spots to meet. They greeted each other with a hug, handshake and then took their seats.

"So papi, what would you like to talk about that's so important?" Carlos asked.

"I can't take that hit you put on Hood and his familia," Byrd said bluntly. Carlos moved slightly up his seat, as if he heard wrong.

"Poppa, explain." He laughed at the sudden change of loyalty. He said nothing but Carlos knew what it was.

"Those are Tech's people, Los, all I want to know is the real reason the death order was made." Byrd didn't budge, but neither did Carlos. They both knew what roles they played in the game, but Carlos wasn't pussy by no means of the word.

"Poppa, who does your loyalty lie with?"

"That shouldn't have to be asked or explained. You already know where my loyalty lies," Byrd assured him.

"So, what the fuck you worried about why the death order was given? Do what I pay you to do. Byrd, we have been through too much for you to pick money over loyalty!" Carlos said, letting his emotions get the best of him.

"What you mean, money over loyalty?" Byrd asked suspiciously.

"Ahh, you thought I wouldn't find out about you going out there and fucking with them bloods? I know all, Byrd."

"Point being what, my nigga? My loyalty has never wavered," Byrd replied angrily.

"Poppa, you right, I'll give you that benefit. The only thing that cuts to my heart is that you won't kill the niggas putting money in your pocket, why? Haven't I treated you good? Like a son?"

"Yeah, Carlos, but it's—" Carlos cut Byrd's words short.

"I see where you and I now stand, poppa. So sad. If you wanted to make money in that form, all you had to do was ask, you know that. But yet you go and bite the hand that feeds you, the hand that feeds you and your baby brother from youth!" Byrd saw it in Carlos's eyes as he got up from the table and walked away.

Byrd remained seated in the same spot, wondering why he let Carlos walk away. He knew he was now a marked man. The executioner was now on the plate to be executed. The irony of the whole situation made Byrd smile, a nervous smile, nonetheless. He got up and left with the mindset of kill or be killed. His mentor was now his next mission. Carlos made his presence felt in the county. The war had begun.

Simfany sat back and witnessed the tragic mayhem take place, damn near between father and son. Byrd was bred to kill, even though the man that took him in and taught him everything was at his head. He had to proceed without emotion. He hated to go against his mentor, he was left with no choice.

Simfany felt the tension in the air every time he came around. She couldn't take it any more, so she spoke her peace. What she didn't want to say was, "I told you so."

"Byrd, sit down and let me talk to you." They were at her townhouse on Edmonson and Carey. Byrd made his way into the living room and took a seat on the edge of one of the loveseats.

"What's up?" he asked.

"Baby, what's going on out there that's making you act like this?"

"My fucking life is being threatened daily by a powerful man. It's only a matter of time before I meet my maker. That nigga taught me everything I know, Simf."

"If you don't mind, what the fuck did you do to Carlos, or what did he do to you?" she asked, not understanding where the bad blood came from.

"After I sold those bricks for you, I opened up shop for myself. Unknowingly, Carlos supplied Hood and his team. Which I really had no way of knowing. Hood Ru bought work from multiple people to maintain his clientele in his hood. He knew about me being one of the suppliers but didn't show that card until it was too late. The old bastard is smart," Byrd laughed, he continued. "He put a bounty on Hood and his familia, but I didn't execute them. He took that as a sign of disrespect and left the meeting angrily. From there on, I knew what it was," Byrd explained.

"Why didn't you kill that nigga when he tried to leave?" Simfany asked, she knew Byrd was slipping.

"That's what I keep asking myself over and over again. That nigga was like my pops, I just couldn't end his career. I also hoped it wouldn't come to this. I didn't play my hand right and now it may lead to my demise." Byrd got up to go upstairs, but Simfany stopped him midway.

"Does he know anything about me?" Byrd couldn't believe his ears. He laughed disappointedly and simply said, "No," as he walked up the steps, knowing after the current visit he wouldn't be coming back.

As the summer approached, Baltimore became a war zone for gangs and turf wars. Byrd continued to hold his own in the streets. Simfany hadn't heard from Byrd since the night they had that conversation concerning Carlos. She was worried about Byrd, but she didn't feel bad though because she told him not to dabble in the drug game. Now he was at war with a man he once loved and respected. As the summer crept in, the chaos over the city died down surprisingly, but only for one reason. One of the main pieces was missing. Byrd! No one had heard or seen him for a matter of weeks.

Simfany worried about his well-being. She went to the only other person she knew would drop everything and ride for Byrd. His little brother Jimmy Parks, aka Jimdog, was the fuck-up between the two and very reckless. A shooter he was, a bitch he wasn't. He was Byrd's shadow, but they were like night and day. While Byrd moved with precision, Jimdog moved with emotion. None of that mattered at the end of the day, all that mattered was finding someone that could find out what happened to Byrd. She knew he would find out or would be ready to put in work to find his brother. Simfany called and let Jimdog know she was on her way to his apartment. She drove to East Baltimore to get answers.

"Yo, what's up, Simf? You straight, shorty?" Jimdog asked as he opened the door of his residence.

"Yeah I'm good, just looking for Byrd. We had a little falling out a couple of weeks ago and I haven't heard from him since. You know where that nigga hiding? I'm starting to get worried." She began to cry. The possibility of Byrd being dead crushed her.

"Shorty, chill, wipe your eyes. I haven't heard from the nigga either, but you know big bro can handle his own," he replied. Simfany sighed. Jimdog obviously didn't know that she could see.

"Jimdog, did you know about the beef between Carlos and Byrd?" she questioned, knowing the answer before it even came out of his mouth. Jimdog was clueless.

"What beef? That nigga love Carlos more than me, why would they be beefing? That sounds crazy, shorty, for real."

"Oh shit, that nigga really didn't tell you about his war with Carlos?" She got hysterical. Simfany was a good actor, she got up from her seat and looked back at Jimdog. It hit her why Byrd didn't tell him. She kept it to herself and tried to walk out. Jimdog was on edge now.

"Hold on, shorty, what are you talking about?" he demanded to know.

"I have to go, Jimmy, I'll explain later when I get the answers to my own questions." Simfany again tried to walk to the door. Jimdog blocked her exit. Instantly, her body was filled with fear.

"What the fuck you mean you about to leave? Bitch, you going to tell me what's going on with my brother!" Simfany moved, trying to get around Jimdog.

"I really don't know too much about the problems him and Carlos had. I don't know the details, I just know they were beefing. I also know it's been the cause of all the bloodshed in the city, niggas been dying left and right. You haven't noticed, nigga? Be real!"

"Bitch, what the fuck you mean?" Jimdog was irate. Simfany was pissed.

"Call me another bitch and you going to lose your fucking tongue. I don't give a fuck who your pussy ass claims to be." Simfany stood her ground.

"Look Simf, I mean no disrespect, but this my blood brother we talking about. I don't know your part in this, but I can sense you know more about this *beef* than you're telling me. Don't let me find out you're involved with this, or that you're holding back on me. You feel me?" Simfany listened to Jimdog speak his peace. The words were going in one ear and out the other.

For the Love of Blood

"Nigga, miss me with the threats. If you hear from Byrd, call me ASAP. Be patient but go find your brother."

"Be safe, Simfany, and I hope I don't hear shit about you in any of this. That's for your best interest. No disrespect intended, but please understand I'm dead serious," Jimdog warned, meaning every word he spoke.

"I fuck with your brother, but what you need to understand is, you put absolutely no fear in my heart. So, you remember *that*, my nigga." She pushed past Jimdog and left the apartment.

***

Months passed, still no word of Byrd. It was driving Simfany crazy not knowing what was going on, she was placed in the middle of all the drama. Simfany had made a monster and she knew it would eventually come back to haunt her in the worst way.

On June 12, Brian "Byrd" Parks was found floating in the Inner Harbor near the ESPN Zone. Simfany grieved over Byrd's death. Jimdog had other issues, he wanted revenge for his brother's spilled blood. Jimdog talked to Carlos over the last couple of weeks since Simfany had left, not sharing all the information. Jimdog didn't want to find out Simfany played a small role in the war that took place. Even though it was a small one, it was a role nonetheless. It was alarming, due to the fact that she tried to hide it. Red flags arose in Jimdog's head.

In all actuality, she did nothing wrong, but if somebody had to take the blame for Byrd's death, it would be her. Carlos explained to Jimdog that he and Byrd squashed the ongoing beef. They stayed away from each other when the truce was set into place. Carlos hadn't heard from Byrd since. Carlos told him that Byrd went back to the county to do his thing as far as business went. What ran through his thoughts daily was, *why would Carlos lie, he is a very powerful man. He had no reason to cop deuces.* Carlos had goons from the states and from overseas willing to put that work in. His reach was long. He was old but was far from pussy, and Jimdog knew that. Being that it left him at odds with who killed his brother and why. Jimdog blamed Simfany, or so that's what he put out.

***

Simfany got wind of what the streets were saying on behalf of Jimdog. She planned to lay low until all was forgotten, or at least until things died down. It didn't take long for that to happen. The streets moved on quickly, but one person didn't forget and let go, Jimdog. He watched and followed Simfany around to see what she did on a daily basis. He followed her for weeks but came up with nothing suspicious. He needed answers.

Simfany was shopping when she recognized Jimdog coming down the aisle. He was vexed, she saw the anger on his face as he approached.

"What's the problem, nigga?" she asked, on point.

"Bitch, you gone tell me what the fuck happened to my brother." Jimdog grabbed Simfany by her hair.

"Ahhhhhh, get off me!" She tried to break his grip, but with no success. Her past had finally caught up to her. He led Simfany out the store and into his Chevy Caprice. To his surprise, she didn't put up much of a fight. *This bitch gangsta,* he thought as he dragged her through the parking lot. He pushed her into the Chevy and pulled off. She remained silent.

"You gone tell me what part you played in my brother's death? The only reason you're still alive is because of the level

For the Love of Blood

of respect Byrd had for you. I don't think you killed him, but you know something and you're not telling me. You will tell me one way or the other. You choose your fate, shorty," Jimdog said as he drove through East Baltimore.

"I don't know anything, Jimdog I can't help you with *who* killed Byrd. I already told you about the war between him and Carlos. What else do you want from me?" she replied, running her fingers through her hair.

"Listen shorty, you gone stop lying to me and tell me what the fuck it is, before I leave you stinking out this bitch. I have a lot of love for you but understand this, I will blow your fucking head off without hesitation. So again, what the fuck happened to my brother, or what do you know? This the last time I'm going to ask you, Simf," Jimdog said, meaning every word. He was known around East Baltimore as being a hot head, but he didn't get all the recognition he deserved because he was Byrd's little brother. He always lived in his brother's shadow unwillingly.

"Byrd let the money get to his head, Jimmy. I gave your brother eight bricks to flip for me. I did it only because I couldn't move that much, but he wanted to. He made a lot of money for knowing the right people. He started fucking with some blood niggas in the county. What part, I really can't say, because I don't remember. I don't know any of their names either. I tried to stay out of that part of the game. All I know is the gang is called TTP, whatever that's supposed to mean. What I do know is he fucked with that bunch of niggas, hard body. Truth is, Byrd was getting gwap, but that's around the time the shit happened between him and Los. Me and your brother weren't on speaking terms, because I told him I didn't want my name to come up in this bullshit involving Carlos. I told Byrd to leave the shit alone, they went hard and went at each other's throats hard. The rest is history. Jim, I loved your brother. I would never do anything to harm him or knowingly let anything happen to him. And when you said the reason I was still alive is because of the love Byrd had for me, that's not it though. I believe the reason I'm still alive is because you know I would never hurt Byrd." Simfany looked forward out the window as her eyes watered.

"Why the fuck you just telling me about this now? Where the fuck you get eight bricks from?" So many different questions ran through his head.

"Before now, none of this was your business. Now about the bricks, some shit happened with my baby daddy that left me straight." Of course, she left out the part about killing Emilio in the process. He looked at her, trying to figure her out.

"So, you don't know none of the niggas' names form the county? As a matter of fact, shorty, what county are you even speaking of, there's a lot of them." *This nigga don't know shit,* she thought.

"I think it's called Harford or some shit like that, I don't know. I don't know about shit but the city. And I barely know much about that," she replied. Jim thought about who he may know out in Harford County. He came up blank at the moment. The only reason he knew niggas from out there is because he was in Hickey with some of them. He was locked up with a couple of them TTP niggas from out that way. A nigga named Blaze who he fucked with hard body was from out there. He made mental note to write Blaze to see if he or his familia fucked with Byrd.

Jimdog drove around with Simfany still in the car, gone off his thoughts.

"Don't leave, shorty, just in case I might need you." He pulled over and let Simfany out. Jimdog pulled off, leaving Simfany at the curb. She cried. Her life was only moments away from being taken away. She promised herself no other nigga would hold that kind of power over her again. Simfany thought that would be the last time she would see Jimdog, but damn she was wrong.

The streets continued to talk, and they weren't speaking in her favor. Simfany had no clue niggas wanted her head she found that out the day of The Stone Soul Picnic. Now, Santana was locked up, facing forever in jail all because of her. If she only knew how pulling that trigger would impact their lives, she would have never done it. Killing Emilio pushed her into another life of danger. A life that now involved the only person she truly loved, her beloved son.

Jamel Mitchell

Chapter 5

Santana woke up in Hickey and thought about what he had done. He ran through what had taken place the week before. He thought daily about his current situation. How he saw it, he wasn't wrong, he was only protecting his mother. No matter what any judge or jury would say. He would always feel like that. Jimdog was a popular nigga in the city, many Baltimore nigga tried to get at Santana on many occasions. He was recovering from a black eye at the moment.

They jumped Santana, but he stood his ground regardless. He stood at five feet tall with the soul of a lion. People had no choice but to respect his G. Santana tried to live as best as possible, he missed his mother most. He didn't want to call collect, but he hadn't talked to her since the night he was booked. He took the time out to call and make sure she was doing okay.

"Hey man, how are you doing? Have you been getting my mail?" she asked as soon as she hit the button to accept his call.

"Yeah, I got your mail. I'm good. What you been up to? I haven't heard from you in weeks," he replied.

"I ain't been doing much, I been out here trying to find you a good lawyer, so these people won't send you away for too long. What's been eating at me is the whole situation even coming down here. You asked to stay, but yet I was stubborn, now you're locked up because of me." Simfany sniffled on the other end of the phone. He could tell it was fucking her up that he was away.

"Once again, Ma, this is not your fault by no means. That dude should have never put his hands on you, point blank. Miss me with that shit," he replied angrily.

"It's more to it than you know, but in time I'll tell you what took place and why," she explained.

"Ight, but when are you going to come and see me?" he blew off her explanation regarding his incarceration.

"You got a court date coming up in a week or so, I'll be there. I'll set up a visit after that. Keep your head up, baby, and know Mommy loves you." Simfany's voice continued to crack.

That hurt Santana deeply, neither one of them could change what happened. He had to live with his actions.

"I love you, pretty lady, I'm good. For real, I'm good. You raised a G. You remember that when you start to worry about me."

"Whatever, boy." She laughed through her silent tears. "Call me whenever, but I'll be at court next week. Love you, Tana."

"Sixty seconds, " the automated voice messaging system interrupted.

"Well, pretty lady, I love you. Please be safe out there. I don't regret pulling the trigger, so don't feel bad. Bye, beautiful." The phone went dead as Simfany tried to reply. Santana got up from the payphone, he looked around at what he gave up for his freedom. He accepted the consequence, so it really didn't bother him that often. The only thing he hated was being away from his mother for so long. She was all he ever had and vice versa. Santana missed being a kid and going to The Key with his friends. Within a couple weeks Santana was forced to become a man. His childhood was over, that he knew for sure. All those thoughts lingered through his head.

He got up and made his way out of the caged dayroom and went to the built-in gym across the hall. He was housed in Unit 3 Clinton Hall, where all the goons of Baltimore resided. It was daily that somebody was bound to get their shit busted.

For the Love of Blood

Today not being any different, at first Santana was the target to everybody's frustration, but that would later change. Santana was respected to a certain extent. He still fought over pulling the trigger on Jimdog; he won some but lost most. But to him, at the end of the day, he wasn't scared to rock with anyone.

Santana entered the gym and sat down near the plastic colorful chairs. Like the ones you see in a children's playroom. Santana watched the TV until he heard a commotion coming from behind him. He turned to see a tall, light-skinned dude arguing with the female staff on duty. She sat at the top of the stairs in a chair. No one but Santana seemed to pay any attention to them.

Everybody but Santana knew Blair, the light-skinned cat, was fucking with that particular C.O. Santana turned his attention back to the TV, he learned fast to stay out of shit that didn't belong to him. The basketball game in the gym caught his attention, nothing was on TV. The game they played was called *50*. He watched as they did their thing while others were just terrible. As the time went by, Blair made his way down the steps and joined the game of *50*. That may have not struck anyone else to be weird, but it struck him as weird. He had never seen Blair pick a basketball up. He couldn't remember at least. He shrugged it off and continued to watch them hoop.

Santana had only taken his eyes off the game for a second when he heard a "thud." It was the sound of someone hitting the ground hard. Blair had snuck Yusuf. Yusuf was a native from the D.C. area, awaiting placement. Yusuf had words with the female C.O. hours earlier. Beyond that, it was known in the streets and behind the g-wall that D.C. and Baltimore weren't fond of each other.

"Pussy, you better watch your mouth when you talk to mine, shorty!" Blair yelled.

Yusuf laid still from the hit, out cold. Blair spit on Yusuf and walked out the gym.

Santana made a mental note. Yusuf stirred, he tried to get up, but he was still punch drunk. Santana got up and walked to the table under the steps and sat on the countertop, it surveyed the whole gymnasium. So, if niggas were to get on some bullshit, he would at least be on point. Yusuf stumbled over to where he was sitting.

"Who hit me, Slim?" Yusuf asked.

"Son, I don't even know. But you good?" Santana answered.

"I know you know, young. Don't feed me that shit, slim. That's that bullshit." Yusuf held his hands on his head.

"Nigga you on ya own with that, I didn't see shit." Santana got up and left Yusuf sitting alone. As Santana walked up the stairs, he was stopped by the female C.O. sitting post.

"I see you know how to keep it G. I'll tell Blair. I'll make sure you're good from now on. Have a nice day, Mr. Vasquez." She smiled and let Santana's arm go. Santana looked back as he walked on. He didn't process what she was saying, so he let it go. As the hours turned into days, niggas began to fall back and left Santana to himself. He obviously observed what was happening, but of course, he still stayed on point.

The day before his day in court, the female C.O. from the other day came back to work. Santana played his distance from her, he saw what could happen if you played with her emotions. While he played his distance, she got closer. She approached Santana during count.

"What's poppin, ma?" he asked, confused. He backed away from the door and as she put her key in and unlocked it. He didn't know what to expect. She looked around before entering his cell. Santana took notice of the action she took.

"Sit down, Santana, I would like to talk to you." He complied and sat down. As he sat down, she leaned against the wall.

"What up, ma?" he asked.

"Nigga, you still don't know my name?" she laughed and shook her head. Santana's face turned red. *Should I know her name?* he thought.

"Nah, never cared truthfully, no disrespect. C.O. was enough for me. Plus, after what I saw a couple of days ago, I probably would've forgot on purpose. I got enough of my own issues. You feel me?" He smiled after the comment.

"Okay, I see you do smile after all," she replied. She moved closer and sat on the bed, only inches away from Santana. She looked at him and smiled.

"I can respect that, but my name is Tijuana." She reached her hand out to dap him up. He reached his hand and showed the same love.

"I told Blair to make sure you were okay from now on. I told him you were my lor brother now and if anything was to happen to you, they would have to deal with me." Tijuana looked Santana in his eyes. "How you feel about that?" she asked, still looking him in his eyes. Santana thought, *damn, ma gangsta.*

"Shit, if it keep these Baltimore niggas off my back, then I'm wit it," he answered truthfully.

"I like the honesty, shorty. How old are you, you look young?" Tijuana asked him.

"Thirteen, but as my familia tells me, that's just a number for one to indicate how much wisdom one has. I'm very mature, thanks to my moms. Being from a big city, it makes you grow up fast."

"Ight, I see you got a little something upstairs. Still young as fuck, but smart." She laughed and pushed him playfully.

She reached into her bra and pulled out a lighter and a small bag of weed. She handed it to Santana.

"What you want me to do with that?" he asked.

"Smoke it, lor nigga. I know you smoke, so miss me with that innocent shit," Tijuana stated firmly.

"You got it, ma, good looking. I appreciate the love."

"Get four or five more years on you and you'll appreciate more than just some weed." She winked at him. She began to leave the room, she stopped in her tracks. "You're lor bro now, so act like it. Be safe, Mr. Vasquez, and do something with that long ass hair." And with that she was gone.

Santana subconsciously rubbed his hands across his head. He looked down at the sandwich bag of weed with the attached white papers.

"What the fuck I'm gone do with this shit?" he asked himself out loud. He laid down. His thoughts were enough to hold him down for the rest of the day.

***

It was the morning of Santana's court appearance. He didn't know what to expect and he didn't know what to say to the judge about his case. *Fuck it*, he told himself. A couple hours later, he was at the Clarence M. Mitchell Jr. Courthouse in downtown Baltimore. He sat in the bullpen in the back, waiting on his name to be called to find out his fate. He was nervous and shaking, thinking about the years he might lose as a child. His heart jumped out of his chest when he heard the bailiff call his name.

"Santana Vasquez!" he called out.

"Santana Vasquez, where are you?" he looked around for someone to acknowledge him. No one responded.

"Santana Vasq ... " his words trailed off as Santana answered.

"I'm here, sorry I didn't hear you the first time, my apologies."

"You ready?" the bailiff asked. Santana nodded his head.

"Okay, come on." He met Santana at the opening of the gate, Santana walked out as the bailiff gave him further instructions.

"Wait here." He locked the gate back. "Put your hands on the wall and spread your legs." He patted Santana down for any contraband. As they began their walk, the bailiff gave Santana more instructions on how to have an easy day.

"My name is Bailiff Lawrence, as most of the kids know me. Since this is my first time seeing you, I'm going to give you a few pointers. Whatever I command you to do, you listen, you understand me?"

"Yeah," Santana replied simply. They had an understanding, so no more was needed to be said. They made the short journey to the courtroom in silence. They two made their entrance through the back room. He walked into the courtroom. He saw at least a hundred people present, a camera crew and the most important person in his life, Simfany. Simfany made eye contact with him, she waved as she wiped the tears away.

Santana was escorted to the left side of the courtroom to the defense table, where his lawyer stood. Simfany did her homework, she hired the best lawyer in the city of Baltimore. Rick Holliver was known for beating murder after murder, many even brutal. Even though his resume was good, Santana had no knowledge of who the man was that stood next to him in his crisp suit and tie.

"Mr. Vasquez, I'm going to be your lawyer through this case, and for any other cases you hopefully don't catch until you are eighteen years of age. Your mother paid a good amount of money to try and get you free today. I'm going to tell you like I told her, you may not go home today or even for a couple of years, but I promise to try my damn best."

"Thank you," Santana replied. He looked back at the crowd for his mother and was surprised to see Carter, Marissa, and Summer. It hurt his heart to see Marissa and Summer crying over him again. He turned around when he felt his eyes getting watery. *I can 't let 'em see me sweat, right?* He laughed at how profound his pride was.

"All rise," Bailiff Lawrence chanted. Everyone in the courtroom rose as the judge walked in.

"Thank you, Mr. Lawrence," the judge stated as she took her seat.

"You may be seated," the bailiff said.

"Court is now in session. I have docket number 02-K-252, State v. Vasquez. Did I pronounce that correctly, sir?" she looked over at Santana.

"Yes, ma'am."

"Okay, moving on. This is the preliminary hearing regarding the defendant, a Mr. Santana Vasquez. According to the docket, he is being charged with attempted murder and felonious assault. Is that correct?" She looked at the prosecutor's table.

"Yes, Your Honor," the assistant prosecutor answered. The judge looked back to the papers sitting in front of her. She shook her head and continued on with the hearing.

"Okay, are there any motions for bond?" she asked the defense.

"As a matter of fact, there is. My client is thirteen years of age. He was born and raised in the cold streets of New York City. But not once did he ever commit any crimes of any kind. So, I ask you Your Honor to please consider that, for this young man to be released to his mother today. He is not a

For the Love of Blood

flight risk, Your Honor, he is a child, an only child. Consider the age and consider this child to go home with his family and friends. If anything, make the bond reasonable for his mother, so she can take her son home where he will be safe. That's all I have, Your Honor. Thank you." Rick walked back to the defense table and sat down.

"Does the State have anything for the defense?"

The female prosecutor stood. "Yes, Your Honor. To those who may not know me, I'm Terry Walker, assistant prosecuting attorney for the D.A.'s office here in Baltimore City. Okay since the pleasantries are out of the way, Judge, I move toward keeping the juvenile in detention. Mr. Vasquez isn't fit to be out on bail, on the grounds that Mr. Vasquez almost ended the life of another human being. Jimmy Parks was left to die in Druid Hill Park. He has too many ties to the New York tri state area. He can very much be a flight risk with the help of an adult." Ms. Walker paused, letting the last comment hang in the balance, a move prosecutors pulled for a jury at trial.

"Your Honor, I ask that he gets no bond until these charges are answered for. That's all I have. Thank you."

"Mr. Holliver, do you have anything else you would like to add?"

"Yes, I do, Your Honor. This is ridiculous, my client is a child that felt he had to protect his mother from grave danger. What the court is trying to make him out to be is unfair on his part. Also, the two charges are almost the exact same charges. It all falls under the same guidelines, not only does it seem that you will most likely not let my client out, but the state is stacking the charges." He looked disgusted. "I would like to make a motion to dismiss the felonious assault."

Mr. Holliver spun around and returned to the defense table. Rick leaned down and whispered into Santana's ear, "We are gonna be alright." He saw the expression on his client's face.

"Ummm .... Okay, let's take a break for ten minutes and come back. Thank you, ladies, and gentlemen. If you can excuse me." The judge got up and went to her chambers. Some spectators left, most stayed put. Mr. Lawrence took Santana to a holding cell in the back of the courtroom, waiting to proceed. Santana knew it broke the hearts of the people that cared about him, but like he told himself a hundred times since he'd been booked, *at any cost I will protect my mother.* They were all they had, he couldn't, and he wouldn't lose her.

Man, fuck... I done did it this time. You fucking idiot! Fuck. He cursed himself as he paced back and forth in the holding cell. The time seemed to slow down as he awaited his fate. The anxiety was killing him. He heard the door unlock and saw Mr. Lawrence coming his way, with his lawyer in tow. Mr. Lawrence unlocked the door to escort Santana back into the courtroom.

"Face the wall, young man, until I open the door. Do not move at any time. Do you understand?" He pushed Santana's head into the wall and held it until he was done talking.

"Yeah, whatever," he replied, pissed that the pussy ass bailiff talked to him in that manner. *I'll kill that nigga if he ever does some shit like that again.* He thought of the bailiff as he was led back into the courtroom. He was getting used to the routine already, that was a bad sign.

"All rise," the bailiff chanted once again. Judge Price made her way back to the bench and took her seat.

"You may be seated."

"Thank you again, Mr. Lawrence. Court is back in session. Docket number 02-K-252. I have the motion to dismiss the felonious assault, am I right, Mr. Holliver?" She looked up at him. He stood.

For the Love of Blood

"Yes, Your Honor."

"Okay, I'm going to grant the motion to dismiss the felonious assault, but of course the murder with intent to kill will still stand. Moving along, Mr. Holliver, how does your defendant plead?"

"Not guilty, Your Honor," Rick answered.

"Okay, do you know how to read and write?"

"Yes, ma'am."

"You understand what's going on today, the date is September 5, 2002?"

"Yes, ma'am."

"You understand your rights regarding your legal counsel?"

"Yes, I do."

"And do you wish to plead not guilty?" Santana got nervous, so he looked back at the only person he could trust. He wanted to know what his mother had to say about it. Simfany was nodding her head yes. She knew what he was thinking before he looked back. He turned around and answered with confidence.

"Yes ma'am, I do wish to plead not guilty."

"State, do you have anything else?" The judge looked over at the prosecutor.

"Yes, we do, Your Honor. Again, I ask that Mr. Vasquez be housed at the Charles H. Hickey School for his safety and ours. That's all I got, Your Honor. Thank you." Ms. Walker took her seat.

"The motion for bond has been denied due to the severity of the crime committed. No matter how old one may be, they must receive the same punishment as everyone else. I'm not indicating you're guilty, but the report is enough to find probable cause. Mr. Vasquez, you will remain in the custody of the Charles H. Hickey School. The next court date will be your trial on these charges. No jury ... I will be the person that judges the trial. So please, Mr. Vasquez, prepare." She looked at the calendar that sat on her desk. "How about after the holidays?" she looked at Rick Holliver.

"That's okay with me and my client, Your Honor. Although I would ask it could be more sooner," he replied.

"How about the state? What's good for you?"

"The date doesn't matter, Your Honor," Ms. Walker stated.

"Okay then, December 5 it is. Mr. Vasquez behave yourself while you're there." She moved on to the next case. The bailiff came to escort Santana back to the bullpen. Santana looked up at the bailiff.

"Can I hug my mother and sisters please, sir?" Mr. Lawrence looked back at the judge to see if she was paying any attention. She was engrossed in the next juvenile's charges. Mr. Lawrence nodded his approval. He walked Santana over to where Simfany and the girls sat. He started with Simfany, she grabbed him and hugged him for what felt like forever. Santana tried to wipe her tears away, but the waist chains hindered him from doing so.

"Pretty lady, I'm good. Remember you raised a G," he told her. He looked up to where Carter stood.

"Stay strong, Tana. Tolerate no disrespect. Let them know you from the Yitty, son."

"Carter!" Simfany exclaimed.

"My bad, ma." He laughed. Santana moved on, coming face-to-face with Summer and Marissa. Their eyes were bloodshot red from all the crying done during the court proceeding.

Summer spoke her peace first, she whispered, "I love and miss you, Santana. I will keep in touch. That I promise." Summer bent and kissed him on his cheek. Last was the love of his

For the Love of Blood

life, other than his mother. Marissa Nunez. As she cried, Marissa grabbed him and kissed him in front of everyone. It fucked Santana up that she was so bold. He instinctively looked over to see if Carter caught the kiss. Carter was smiling, it was obvious he knew what was going on.

"I already told him about us. He said he approved, just put it like that. He has no problem with us being together. When you left, I couldn't eat, sleep, or focus in school. I was having withdrawals. I miss you so much, Santana. Please be good in there, Santana, so you can come home early." Mr. Lawrence grabbed the crook of Santana's arm, letting him know it was time to go.

"I love y'all, I'm good. You guys keep your heads up. Don't worry about me. I'm doing fine." He left the courtroom without looking back.

Santana was taken back to Hickey that night, but instead of being placed back on Clinton Hall, he was put in segregation, only with the notion that he had to see administration before he could be released. Santana was tired and pissed. He kicked the door at his full potential until he was broke down and too tired to continue. No one came. The doors were kicked on a regular, so it was nothing out of the ordinary to hear the loud banging of metal. The room was filthy; he cleaned it to the best of his ability and succumbed to his restlessness.

***

Boom ... Boom ... Boom ... Santana stirred. The banging woke him from his sleep.

Boom ... Boom ... Boom ... The banging was coming from his own door. He looked up to see a C.O. waiting at his door.

"Vasquez, get up, the admin wants to meet with you!" the C.O. yelled through the door.

Boom ... Boom ... the C.O. banged again just to be a smart ass.

"Ight nigga, chill. I'm up!" he yelled back.

"Yeah aight, lor nigga, hurry the fuck up then. The motherfucking admin board is waiting on you." That was the last thing the C.O. said before he walked off. Santana got up and brushed his teeth, combed his hair and wrapped it into a ponytail. He looked at his bed in an attempt to make it but changed his mind. He waved it off. *Fuck that shit.* He walked up to the door and tried to look out his window. He was too short, so he settled for banging on the door. He waited for the arrogant officer to appear, but he didn't. He was livid. He started to kick the door with all his might.

Boom ... Boom ... Boom ... Boom ... The banging grabbed the attention of the staff. The same officer that woke Santana minutes before, stood at the door with a screw face.

"Kick the door again, lor nigga, and I'm going to fuck you up," he said, meaning every word. The Hickey School was known for the violence the staff and inmates caused. So, the threat didn't fall on deaf ears.

"I know that's right, son. I'm ready, *Officer.*" The C.O. opened the door and Santana walked out. He stood between the bullpen and the showers, awaiting his next order. When the C.O. was done locking the door back, he walked off, Santana followed.

This bitch ass nigga think I'm some kind of fucking dog, he thought as he followed the correctional officer up the hall. The C.O. took him up front to the control room so he could go behind the fence to Clinton Hall. Santana saw the van that awaited him. The van was blue with steel gates as its windows. The van was extremely old. Santana hopped in the van and the air hit him, soothing his anger a little.

For the Love of Blood

The housing units outside the fence were known as the Impact Programs. They really didn't pay much attention to the inmates. It was a lot freer on the *Impact* side of things. The Impact Program was designed for people with thirty-, sixty-, and ninety-day commitments. Santana knew he wouldn't be so lucky, but he still held onto the hope. As the van pulled up to the curb of Clinton Hall, they were met by an older white female. Sister Pat was the child advocate of the jail. She was in the presence of another staff member.

"How are you doing, sir? Have you been okay since you've been here?" Sister Pat asked as they walked up the walkway.

"Yes, ma'am. I'm doing fine," he replied in the same voice he talked to his mother with.

The innocence was still there. It was dim, but it was still there.

"Okay, we have a meeting today. If you don't want to talk, you don't have to. So, don't feel pressured," she explained.

"Thank you, Sister Pat." She nodded a smile as he opened the door for her. The unit was locked down, the pair of tables set up in the middle of the multipurpose room he guessed was the reason. He looked at the people that stared at him. Out of all the faces, he only recognized one, Tijuana's. And she wasn't on the panel, she was present as the staff member on duty. She blew Santana a kiss and waved. Her gesture put Santana at ease.

"This way, Mr. Vasquez," the segregation officer ordered. He led Santana into the multipurpose room. The room was used for the inmate meals, card games, telephone calls, and more likely than all, fights. Santana took his seat and waited for the administration to explain why he was put in segregation.

"Good morning, darling. I'm Sister Pat, the child advocate for the facility." She introduced herself as if it was the first time they met.

"Mr. Vasquez, my name is Roger Blackwell and I'm the assistant warden here at the facility."

What the fuck did I do to get the warden here? he asked himself.

"Mr. Vasquez, good morning to you. I'm Harper Riley, the internal investigator here at Hickey." He reached over the table to shake Santana's hand. They shook hands.

"I know you haven't been here that long, so I'll have the staff introduce themselves as well," Mr. Riley stated.

"Hi, Mr. Vasquez, my name is Tijuana Moore. I'm a correctional officer here at the facility also, nice to meet you."

"My name is Green and I'm also an officer at this facility." Santana laughed at the corny ass introductions.

"Now, the reason you are here today is because of the contraband we found in your room while you were at court. Anyway, can you explain where you got it from?" Mr. Riley asked.

"Nah, I just had it, I guess." Santana stated as little as possible.

"I don't believe you came into this facility with drugs, so I will ask you again. Where did you get the contraband? Who brought you the contraband in?" Riley asked with a slight bit of irritation in his voice.

"Son, I already told you, I had it with me the whole time. If you choose not to believe me, it is your problem. Now, can I go?" Santana held eye contact with the investigators with no sign to back down.

"Listen, I'm not trying to be a hard ass or anything like that and if it seems that way, I apologize. But this is a serious matter and whether you cooperate or not, we will handle this. Right now, you're facing a couple of years in segregation for this, so make your choice." Santana laughed at Riley's comment.

"I already told you, Mr. Riley the investigator, so I have nothing more to say regarding this matter. By the way, I'm young at the age of thirteen, but my mother didn't raise a fool. So, with that 'a couple years' stuff, miss me with that. If you can take me back to my cell for the next two days, I would appreciate it. After that, you have to let me out, per the governor of Maryland." Santana sat up in his chair at attention. He was happy he might have defeated the tough asshole.

"Mr. Green, you can escort Mr. Vasquez to his cell in lockup. Have a nice day, sir." Santana stood, maintaining eye contact with Tijuana. She smiled. He didn't cease to amaze her. As he made his way through the room he stopped and turned back to the panel of people.

"If this goes any further, I ask that you contact my lawyer and my mother, because I won't speak to you about this topic again." He went to exit the room but was stopped by Riley this time.

"And who might your lawyer be, Mr. Vasquez?" he asked, being a smart ass.

"His name is Rick Holliver, the third. Baltimore's best." And with that, he left with C.O. Green. Nothing more was to be said from either party, because everyone knew who Pretty Ricky was. Santana was led to the van.

"Damn shorty, I see you showed your ass in there." Green laughed. What he didn't know was that Santana was shaking nervously. That meeting scared the shit out of him. The people in the meeting were important people. Going at the investigator like that might have sealed his fate at Hickey. He couldn't do a year in the hole, that's for sure, but he called Riley's bluff. No matter the offense, besides escape, as a child you could only do three days max in segregation. He heard it, so he ran with it, surprisingly it was true indeed. He relaxed in the back of the van as he went to his confinement in segregation.

Chapter 6

As Simfany sat in her home in West Baltimore, she thought about Santana. She thought about Byrd also. She thought strongly about who could be responsible for Byrd's death, if Carlos didn't kill him. Jimdog said Carlos admitted to stopping the war between the two and became partners. There was money to be made, but she wasn't falling for that bullshit. She didn't know who was lying, Jimmy or Carlos. Carlos had no reason to lie, but at the end of the day, he lost money when he went to war.

She also thought how easy it would be for Carlos to just kill Jimmy if he wanted. That was the only thing that stopped her from thinking Carlos was responsible for Byrd's death. It confused and frightened her, to say the least.

At the moment, Santana was her main focus. Her baby boy was only thirteen and from what the judge said yesterday, he was facing an ass load of time if convicted. She didn't know if it was a good thing or a bad thing that Jimmy survived. She asked God every night why he couldn't sacrifice Jimdog's life for Santana's. Jimdog put a little fear through her veins also. The only thing working in her favor was the fact that no one knew where she lived, but she wouldn't be hard to find if they looked for her. That she knew.

When she saw Santana in his gray's, it killed her internally. She was proud of him also because he showed her he would do anything to protect her. She loved him very much and was now lost without him. They were a team of their own. The argument they had over moving she thought she lost him. She made a pact within herself when Dracula got killed, that it would be them against the world. Not having Santana around had her losing her mind. It haunted her to let the past go, but she couldn't stop dwelling on the past. The vision of

Santana as a baby is what got her through so many occasions. Yeah, it was official, Simfany was depressed and losing her marbles.

After soaking in her memory, she decided to cook something to make herself feel better.

She walked over to her stereo entertainment system and put Jay-Z's *Blueprint* album in the CD deck. She turned to her favorite song by Hov, *Song Cry*. While she listened to Jay-Z spit the truth, she went into the kitchen and pulled out a frozen steak and some instant potatoes. She sang along as she sat the steak in the sink to thaw. *"Can't see them coming down my eyes so I gotta let the song cry ... Good dude, I know you love me like cooked food even though a nigga had to move like ..."*

The words touched deep in her heart as she continued to sing along. She moved around the spacious townhouse. She started to clean the living room waiting for the steak to unthaw. While she was in the living room fluffing the pillows on the sofa, she heard a knock at the door.

"Who is it?" she asked after she put the pillow back in its place. She got no answer.

"Who the fuck is that at my door!" she yelled out again, getting ghetto and irate. She walked to the door and looked out the peephole. She saw a sexy nigga with dreads standing on the porch under the bright light.

"What do you want?" she asked through the door. She remained on her tiptoes, looking through the peephole at the man's body language. There were no signs of aggression.

"I'm a friend of Byrd's, shorty. He told me if l ever needed anything to holla at his wife, Simfany," the man stated from the other end of the door.

"And you are?" she asked, getting curious about the young man standing on her porch. What she wanted to know was

For the Love of Blood

how he knew where she lived and where he knew Byrd from? Maybe he had answers she needed.

"My name is Stacks, shorty. I come in peace. I gotta holla at you, Simfany. It pertains to the death of Byrd. I think I know who killed him." The accent he possessed was slightly different from a Baltimore accent, it was a name and accent she would never forget.

"Give me a second to put some clothes on."

"Ight, shorty." She watched as the teenager sat down on the steps and waited. She ran upstairs and grabbed her Glock 17 with an extra clip. She kicked her slippers off and put on some sneakers. *Just in case this nigga on some bullshit.* She shook her head, she sounded like Byrd. Byrd had taught her well. Before she left the room, she looked at the bulletproof vest she had hanging in the closet, the one Byrd had brought her, she shrugged it off. If she needed protection, she had it in her grips. She descended down the stairs with a head full of confusing thoughts, but it was better to be safe than sorry. That she knew from experience.

If this nigga knows where I live, Byrd must have told him something. I got something for this nigga if he thinks about crazy. She hyped herself up. Before she was face-to-face with the door again, she checked the clip to make sure it was full. The magazine was full. She unlocked the door with the Glock resting against her back. If she was tripping, she would put the gun away, but she was always taught to act with precaution, especially since she had a date with her own demons. Simfany unfastened the chain link and unlocked both top and bottom bolts. She opened the door slowly.

"Nigga, this shit better be good." She lost her voice when she saw the nigga on the porch with his gun pulled. She tried to swing her arm around to up her own strap, but it was too late.

The teen opened fire. *Boc... Boc... Boc...* Simfany fell back against the railing of the steps, trying to hold her balance from the impact of the bullets. She coughed, spewing up blood. She willed to raise her Glock again. She felt the impact from two more slugs before she fell into darkness.

After the shots dropped Simfany to the ground, Stacks walked into the townhouse and looked at a dying Simfany and smiled. She was covered in her own blood, his favorite color. Stacks aimed the gun at Simfany's face and squeezed the trigger one last time. The blood poured out of Simfany at a rapid speed. Stacks reached into his back pocket and pulled out a navy-blue bandana, he leaned over and dropped it on her face. He walked out of the townhouse and hopped into a new green Altima and drove off, leaving Simfany in a fight for her life.

***

"Blatttt... Blatttt.... Blllaattttttt..." was all Santana heard as he woke up in the hole yet another night. Most of his niggas was Va-Holla, so he knew the call all too well. He knew when a blood nigga was in the building. As he wiped the cold out his eyes, the person continued on screaming his gang lingo.

"Blllllaaaaaaaaaaatttttttttttttt." Santana walked up to the door and began to jump to see out the cell window, but with no luck. He saw no one. He tried multiple times, but still didn't see anyone. He got down and looked under the door to see if anyone was moving around in the bullpen. Still, he couldn't see anybody.

"Blatttttttt!" Then the bullpen cage started to rattle. *Boom... Boom... Boom...* The person in the bullpen continued to kick the cage.

"What's poppin, son?" Santana yelled under the door.

"Who dat, blood?" the voice on the other side of the door questioned.
"Santana!"
"Santana who yo?"
"Santana Vasquez, my nigga," Santana spoke with pride.
"And who the fuck is that? What hood you from, shorty?"
"Courtlandt Ave."
"Where dat homie?"
"New Yitty."
"Oh yeah, what you say your name was again, lor yo?"
"Santana."
"Oooooh, you the lor niggas that blasted that bitch ass nigga Jimdog?"
"I guess, if that's how you wanna put it. That's what the D.A.'s saying."
"Damn dog, what you doing back here? Don't tell me you scared to live on the complex, shorty?"
"Nigga, hell nah. You got me fucked up, my G. They found some weed in my cell when I went out to court," he explained.
"I was just fucking with you though, shorty. The nigga Blair fuck with you hard body, which is some new shit because the nigga usually don't fuck with no one. Heard you went hard for yours. The heart of a lion as I like to call it."
"I been hearing that a lot lately. I just live how I was taught to, my nigga. Win, lose or draw, you feel me? What's ya name though, son?"
"Rolando, Rolando Dempsey. I bang that T.T.P. 400 block Spruce Street, West Side all day till my casket drop, White Lock City where I was born and bred," Rolando announced.
"Damn son, you on ya shit hard. That's what's good, my nigga. Most of my familia is Va-Holla, you ever heard about them?" Santana yelled under the door.

"One of the big homies was telling me about some shit them lor niggas started out there in the Bronx, that where you from, shorty?"

"Yeah, what you booked for?"

"Me and my lor banked this nigga from over East, fucked the lor nigga up too. Crab ass nigga kept running his mouth," Rolando said with pride as if it was the best achievement in the world. Santana could hear the keys in the distance as they approached. The door to the segregation unit was opened. Santana hurried up and dusted himself off. He could hear the keys, but he couldn't see anything. He was the only one in the hole, so if they were back here, then they were there to get him or Rolando.

"Damn shorty, you real mean with that switch," Rolando said as Tijuana passed by. She walked up to Santana's door and she looked in and saw him smiling back at her. *I'm going to hate to tell this nigga about his mother.* She shook her head and smiled back. She unlocked the door and walked into the room, leaving the door wide open. Santana walked up to her and hugged her. She knelt down to embrace him. He was happy to see a familiar face.

"Lor man, sit down, I gotta talk to you about something very important. First off, thank you for having my back on the weed situation." Tijuana smiled, showing off her pearly whites.

"It ain't nothing, ma. It's all love, you know that," he replied as he stood near the combined toilet and sink. Tijuana patted at the mat for Santana to come and take a seat. When he went and sat down, he thought he saw a tear rolling down Tijuana's face. *I'm trippin'*, he told himself.

"Baby boy, please be calm and hear me out." She grabbed his hands and looked him in his eyes.

"Ma, what's good? You can tell me, I won't spazz," he said sincerely.

"Baby, your mother was shot last night and she not looking good ... I" her words trailed off as Santana went numb. His mind couldn't process what she just had told him. He could see her mouth was still moving, but no words seemed to come out. He came back to reality to hear her still talking. "I don't know, but that was all that was said."

"What you just say?" he asked with tears welling in his eyes, then it all came back to him, fast and hard. "My mother is dead?" He got hysterical. "What the fuck you mean, my mother is dead!" he cried harder. "Tijuana, she can't be, please, ma, tell me this a joke," he begged. Tijuana cried for Santana. His pain was starting to get unbearable for her to watch. He was still a child, and you could still see the innocence in his face as he cried. *Just a child,* she told herself.

"She's not dead, but she is badly hurt, Santana. She was shot six times and left for dead. They found her at her townhouse, barely breathing. She was draped in some kind of blue linen. It was placed across her face," she explained through her own tears. He laid his head in her chest and cried for what seemed like hours. *His mother's the only person in the world that mattered to him, now that's threatened to be taken away.* He couldn't fathom that. They sat there so long he eventually cried himself to sleep. Tijuana laid him down and left the room. She looked back at Santana curled upon his mat.

"I love you, Santana."

"I love you too, pretty lady," he said in his sleep, subconsciously thinking she was his mother. Tijuana knew that was Santana's nickname for Simfany. It broke her heart to see him hurting, but there was nothing she could do about it. She locked the cell door back and left. She wiped her tears away as she walked through the segregation unit.

"Yo shorty, lor homie aight in there?" Rolando asked as if he was concerned.

"No, family issues. Tragic situation, when he wakes up, he is going to need somebody there to talk to. I know you don't know the lor nigga but show him some love." She walked out the door to the main control area.

***

Detective Ramos walked into the hospital and shook his head. He hated the smell of hospitals. His partner, Detective Lawson received the call of a shooting that took place over in West Baltimore. No witnesses, as usual. So, the detectives were starting from scratch like every other case they came in contact with. All they knew at the moment was the victim in the shooting was a woman approximately in her early thirties, with six gunshot wounds in multiple areas. The detectives walked together to the check-in desk at Bon Secours hospital located on West Baltimore Street.

"Hi, I'm Detective Ramos, and this is my partner Detective Lawson." Lawson nodded at the secretary. Ramos continued. "We're here investigating the shooting of..." he looked down at the papers he carried in. "A Simfany Vasquez. Can you lead us in the right direction of her room please?" The secretary picked the phone up and called the floor Simfany was being held on.

"Sorry, but she would be no use to you right now. She is in surgery as we speak. Again... I'm sorry, Officer," the secretary said politely.

"When she wakes up, can you or her doctor please give us a call? Here are my and my partner's cards. Thank you, sweetheart," he said, handing the secretary two business cards. The detectives walked out of the hospital and went home. There was nothing that could be done that night. It was now a waiting game if she survived. It was days before either detective got a call from Simfany's doctor at Bon Secours. The detectives made their way to room 220, where Simfany was housed, in the ICU ward. Simfany was doing better, but not good enough to be alone. So, they kept her close, at least until she was ready to be on her own without worry. They walked into the room as quietly as possible.

As they entered, they saw two Baltimore transportation officers and a young man dressed in orange coveralls. He was also shackled and handcuffed. The young man obviously didn't hear them come in, and he showed no signs if he did. They walked up close enough to overhear what he was saying through his sobs.

"Ma ... I swear to God, I'm gone kill the nigga that did this to you. Please pull through .... Please pull through, pretty lady. I can't live without you," the boy cried. The detectives looked at each other. They didn't know Simfany Vasquez had an incarcerated son. Detective Ramos made a mental note to check into who the child was.

"Know I love you, pretty lady, and I'll die before this shit happens again." The detectives could tell he meant every word.

"I love you, Tana, stay out of trouble for me please." She barely could speak. It was more of a whisper than anything. Santana leaned in and kissed Simfany on the cheek. Detective Ramos then made his presence known.

"Excuse me." He waited to catch the attention of all in the room. Santana looked back through bloodshot eyes. Simfany looked up toward the detectives.

"I apologize, but I'm Detective Ramos." His partner followed up behind him on cue.

"And I'm Detective Lawson." He nodded his head.

"We're here to ask you about the shooting that took place four nights ago," Ramos said, looking for a response of some kind. Not getting one, he moved on.

"I understand, this is your mother. I'm clueless as to what your name is and why you are incarcerated in the Hickey School." Santana looked at the transportation officers to see if he had to answer the question. They shrugged their shoulders, basically telling him he could if he wanted to. Santana looked at the detectives up and down, he turned back to his mother's bedside. He bent down and kissed her again before he was escorted out the room, back to Hickey.

"Ma' am… again, we are here to help, so please help us catch the person who did this to you," Detective Ramos pleaded.

"Officer truthfully, I didn't see the guy's face who shot me. I remember little," she whispered.

"Okay, we gone play like that? What about the Glock 17 they had to pry out of your hand? Explain that, Ms. Vasquez," Detective Lawson blurted out.

"Talk to my lawyer if you're going to charge me with anything. His name is Mr. Ricky Holliver," she spoke softly. "I need my rest as you can see, so if you don't mind, can you please leave me to do just that," she stated, then turned her head the other way looking out the hospital window. Tears continued to fall down her face. The detectives were leaving when Lawson stopped. He wanted to ask one more question.

"What is your son's name, if you don't mind?" she mumbled something, but neither detective could understand what she was trying to say.

"Excuse me, ma'am, I'm sorry. I didn't hear you." Lawson moved closer.

"Santana Vasquez, now please leave."

For the Love of Blood

"Again ma'am, I'm sorry for bothering you. we'll be in touch. If you can remember anything—"

"Leave please." Before they left, each detective slyly put their cards down on the telephone stand.

Detective Ramos walked out of the building confused. They had a beautiful woman laid up in the hospital with six bullet wounds that was close to taking her life and she didn't want any help. *She was scared that anyone could see, but it was clear she didn't want any help. The no-snitch policy was getting out of control.*

Detective Lawson stopped before he got into the marked car, the look of confusion plastered on his face as well. *Santana Vasquez ... Santana Vasquez ... where do I know that name from?*

"Aye, Ramos, what does the name Santana Vasquez mean to you?" he looked over the hood of the car and asked.

"I'm drawing blanks. I swear, I know I heard that name before too. But like I said, I can't remember where," Ramos explained.

"I gotta look into it. That boy is too young to be locked up," Lawson said.

"Shit, you never know it may help us with our case. Most likely it won't, but it's worth a shot. Simfany is obviously not going to cooperate. I hate the no-snitch mentality," Ramos expressed his feelings to his partner about the street code of conduct. Both detectives sat in silence as Ramos drove back to the precinct. The name Santana Vasquez lingered in the back of both of their minds.

As Ramos parked the car, Lawson made his way through the precinct. He said his hellos as he beelined for his desk. He sat for a minute, again he thought about the name in question. *I know I heard that name from somewhere before, but from where?* he asked himself over and over. He came up blank for the umpteenth time.

"Fuck it," he said as he logged on to his computer. He typed in the name, *Santana Vasquez.* He was a juvenile charged with attempted murder with the intent to kill. He finally remembered where he heard the name. He was the shooter of Jimmy Parks at the Stone Soul Picnic.

"I'll be mother fucking damned," Lawson said, looking at the connection between the infamous Parks family and Vasquez pair. It couldn't get any realer. *Simfany, you embarked on the wrong journey, sweetheart.* He told himself as he did more research. Lawson got up to show his partner, knowing he wouldn't believe him unless he'd seen it with his own eyes.

***

Santana arrived back at Hickey no later than 3:00 pm, just in time to eat dinner. He was still shaken after seeing his mother in so much pain. The doctor said she was shot six times in all. She was shot once in her stomach, twice in her chest cavity, once in her thigh, once in the arm and once in the neck. Even though she was in better condition today than before, he was still in fear of losing his mother. He hadn't personally known his father, but he felt like now was the time *they* needed him the most. Santana loved his father, despite not knowing him. He heard about who he was and what he was about, other than the stories, it was nothing. Little did Santana know he held many of the same traits his father possessed. All those thoughts ran through his head as he sat in the dayroom in Clinton Hall. He was kind of hungry and wanted to eat, but he just didn't feel up to the task.

For the Love of Blood

"Aye lor, yo, you gone eat that tray, dog?" Some random ass nigga seated at the table asked. Santana looked at the boy sitting next to him, he had never seen the light-skinned, buck toothed boy before. He screwed his face at the question.

"I don't even know you, son. I'm not giving you my shit, my nigga," Santana replied, looking the boy in his eyes.

"Dog, who you think you talking to, shorty?" He stood up looking down on Santana.

"Manley, sit your ass down!" C.O. Green shouted from inside the cage. Manley sat down, but he knew he made his point. Manley stood at five-eight, a hundred and eighty-five pounds. But Santana didn't care about how big he was, or how big he thought he was. Something had to be done to restore his security.

He knew he couldn't let that issue slide. He looked over and Manley was seated and eating again. He looked at Santana and smiled. Santana looked down when he caught *his* gaze. Manley took *his* eyes off Santana for a split second and was caught with a two-piece, surprising *him.* Santana was now on *his* feet, feeding the boy all he had. Manley quickly covered up enough to push Santana away.

They squared up for the fair one. Santana played back and waited on Manley to swing, Manley had too much weight on *him* for Santana to rush attack. But on the other hand, Manley used *his* weight to *his* advantage and rushed Santana into the corner of the pod near the blue collect phones.

Santana was stuck in a hard place with nowhere to go. He was stuck against a cage and in a way he was helpless. Manley caught *him* with a vicious blow to the side of his face and head. He swung the best he could, the hits were so clean to his face, he had no choice but to curl up against the fence the best way he could. Manley hit him one last time before he stopped. Santana was too dizzy from the blows to understand what was going on. His face was bloody and swollen. As he wobbled back to his tray, he began to regain his vision and heard more commotion coming from behind him.

He jumped up and turned around to square up again. But as he saw this time, Manley was on the losing end. Without a second thought, Santana ran over to the fight and jumped in. He kicked and punched Manley. Manley was punch drunk trying to run from the pair. He didn't have much space to run to, they were locked inside of a cage. Manley collapsed at the door where the food was served only twenty minutes prior and curled up into the fetal position.

"That's enough!" C.O. Stone called out through the cage. Santana and the stranger continued to stomp on Manley until the staff ran in and broke the fight up.

"Lor nigga, I said that's enough," Stone yelled as he jogged to break the fight up. Manley was a smart ass, so he wasn't liked much in Hickey, but the boy had them hands. So, he wasn't tested much. That was probably one of the reasons they didn't hurry to break the fight up. He needed an ass whooping they couldn't give. Stone grabbed Santana and the other inmate and walked them to the back of the unit. The stranger that rode for Santana started screaming.

"Touch him again, nigga… flat out! Touch him again." He was trying to break out of Stone's grip.

"Y'all lor niggas did y'all thing, chill the fuck out," Stone said as he walked them down the hall. They were locked into a cell together.

"Y'all niggas sit back here and cool down." Santana mugged the C.O.

"Fuck you."

"Nah, fuck you, lor nigga." Santana smiled at the C.O.'s lame ass.

For the Love of Blood

"You a bitch nigga, I been heard about you. At least I'll take my ass whoopin', you not so much." Stone advanced into the room. Santana stood his ground and didn't budge. The other inmate stepped in.

"Chill cuz, the lor nigga trippin' right now. Let him live, shorty." Stone glared at Santana, he wanted to say something, but he turned and left. When Stone left the room, neither of them spoke two words to one another. The minutes passed with no conversation making the situation awkward. C.O. Green walked up to the doorway with two trays in his hands.

"Y'all want the rest of your food?" he asked both boys. They walked to Green and got their trays. Without another word Green turned and left, leaving the door open this time. Santana sat in the corner of the room near the caged window, and slowly began to eat. He looked up at the nigga that could have possibly saved his life.

"Son, you want half of this? Ain't no way I'm going to be able to eat all this. It hurt to get the shit down. That nigga Manley fucked my jaw up. It feels like it might be broken, son," he explained as he held his hand to his face and moved his jawbone from side to side.

"Nah, I'm good, shorty. Eat your food," was all the stranger said to Santana as he finished eating his own tray. Santana went back to playing with his food. He wanted to, and tried to eat, but the pain was just too much. He stubbornly pushed the tray away from him. Santana sat on the floor and waited for the dude on the bed to stop eating before he started with all his questions.

"What's ya name, my G?" Santana asked anyway.

"Drew ... all my niggas back home call me Drew," he replied.

"My name Santana, I appreciate you back there. He was starting to do damage. He woulda probably killed me if they let him." Santana smiled but thought better of it because of the soreness of his jaw. The whole thing was just funny to him.

"Where you from, my G?"

"I'm from Aberdeen ... Washington Park to be exact," he answered with pride.

"No disrespect, fam, but where is that? I'm not from Baltimore. I'm from the Yitty."

"Ain't no disrespect taken, lor yo. I know where you from. Niggas talk, I also know you bang for yours. So, of course, I respect that. Especially from a nigga so small and young, you got heart, my dude. I couldn't just watch that nigga smash you like that. And my hood located in Harford County. It's like forty-five minutes away from the city. I live in the projects, right behind the Amtrak on Route 40. You ever been there? Probably not. But like I said, that's my hood. A lot of these Baltimore niggas underestimate county niggas, but we bang just as hard, if not harder." Santana nodded. Drew had Santana's full attention.

"Again, good looking, son. I owe you one."

"Never owe no one shit, lor yo, just remain loyal and I got you," Drew said.

"That's love. Word on my raise, I got you."

"Ain't no need to put anything on your peoples. Just show and prove, shorty. You feel me?" Drew asked, making sure Santana understood him.

"Yeah," Santana replied, holding his jaw.

"Now shut up and let your face heal." They both laughed, forming a bond that would never be broken till death.

Chapter 7

In a project complex deep in the heart of the Bronx, Justice sat on the hood of a parked car. Ever since Santana had left, he lost his head. Santana was like his brother, and he missed him daily. Even though he still had Peewee, nowadays, even Peewee was missing in action. He barely stayed in Melrose anymore. There was no reason to. Both his niggas were MIA. Justice was lost in thought when Bogus pulled up.

"What's popping, blood? You look like you out here gone. Hop in, we gotta talk about ya brother," Bogus explained through the window of his 2002 Mercedes Benz. Without a response, Justice hopped off the parked car to get in with Bogus. Bogus was the first command in Va-Holla.

It was the Blood gang for the up-and-coming soldiers, it was the stage of life where they showed their loyalty most. On the other hand, Bogus was official homie under the sex, money, murder banner. He just wanted to keep his Va-Holla homies on point, so he remained loyal to them also. Justice entered the car and slouched in the passenger seat. He and Bogus did their Va-Holla handshake as soon as they got situated.

"What's poppin, son? What brings you down this way?" Justice asked.

"I looked for you in the hood, but ya little girlfriend told me you was up this way. Did you hear about what happened to ya familia?"

"Yeah, son been bagged for a grip. I forgot to tell you that. That shit got me out here losing my mind for real, you know that's my right, my nigga."

"I know, son, but I came to talk to you about Simfany. They just tried to murder her last week in Baltimore." Bogus let the news of Simfany sink in.

"Hold up, nigga, what the fuck you mean? Bogus, what the fuck are you talking about?" he got hysterical. Simfany was like his second mother. He was willing to kill a block for that lady, so to hear the news of her being shot had him feeling some type of way. It angered him, but it crushed him more than anything. A lone tear rolled down his face as he thought of the harm that came upon Simfany.

"Son, she gone?" Justice asked the question he really didn't want to know the answer to.

"Nah, she pulled through, but she still fucked up. She was shot six times, so she is going to need protection. I think you should go to Baltimore for her."

"My nigga, you know how I feel about my lady, but I'm still only thirteen, my nigga. There isn't much I can do to protect her. I'm not talented enough with that ratchet, in all honesty. Don't get me wrong, I got the heart to rock and burn anything or anybody I just don't know exactly what I'm doing when it comes to niggas that really play that ratchet game."

"I don't understand that, but you gotta put that thirteen-year-old shit in a box. It don't matter how old you are, get your mind right, little nigga. Ya peeps need you, son," Bogus said. He was disappointed in the second guessing of Justice's mental. Justice was the nigga that always came to him willing to put work in for him. Fighting was defiantly different than murking niggas, that's for sure. It seemed like Justice could read Bogus's mind, so he spoke on it.

"Don't think I'm second guessing anything, big bro. I'm just not trying to get me or Simfany killed. I can't protect Simfany if those Baltimore niggas put me in a sandbox. Think about that, bro, what good can I do then?" Justice sat up and spoke his mind to the best of his ability. He looked Bogus in his eyes.

"I understand, little man. Be safe out here, these Morehouse niggas don't have much love for Courtlandt Ave. Stay 050, little bro."

"Ight, you know where I rest my head if you need me. Remember what I said about not knowing that murder game like that. But with help, I can learn quickly," he said, putting a lot of emphasis into quickly. He dapped Bogus up and got out of the Mercedes. Justice's mind ran wild over the information he just received. He watched as Bogus pulled off. He promised himself that he would learn how to really use his gun. The day Bogus left Justin on the block would be the last day Justice would ever second guess any of his actions.

***

Simfany was released from the ICU and put into a regular room. She was showing great improvement, grateful to be alive after the ordeal. Every time she attempted to move her body, it ached badly. While she was in the hospital, she made a vow to herself that she would never go through the same kind of pain twice. The only thing she could recall was the sound of a gun and the dreads the shooter had. Simfany tried hard to remember the face of the shooter, but she kept coming up blank. It hurt her more than the actual shells to let Santana see her so fucked up. But what could she do? Nothing. It was out of her hands.

The thought of revenge ran through her head every second of the day. But again, she was always faced with the fact that she didn't know who pulled the trigger. All she knew for sure was it had something to do with Byrd's death, or so she assumed. The continuous murderous thoughts ran through her head was enough to declare war on every Baltimore nigga moving. Simfany calmed down, she reached over and grabbed the phone out of its cradle. She dialed the number she knew all too well, but never had to call.

"¿Cómo estás?" a solemn voice answered.

"I need you. I was shot and left for dead," she cried into the phone.

"Where are you?" the man asked in a deep Latin accent.

"Baltimore City."

"Say no more, Chula, be safe. I come soon." And the phone went dead, bringing their conversation to an end. Simfany looked at the phone and then hung it up. A smile crept across her face as she laid back and relaxed for the first time in a week. The thought of what was to come to the city of Baltimore had her hype. Simfany was about to make the city of Baltimore rain blood. Little did she know, Simfany Vasquez's blood was no different than anybody else's.

It was on now ...

***

Detective Ramos was the leading D.T. in the shooting of Brian "Byrd" Parks a couple of months ago. No witnesses, no evidence, no trace of a crime besides the murdered victim. Ramos was looking at the case becoming a cold one, until the case of Simfany Vasquez came across his desk. There was some kind of connection between the two he couldn't yet figure out. Yeah, he knew Santana was responsible for the shooting of Jimmy Parks, Byrd's little brother. But the question he continued to ask himself ... *beyond that, what connection did they have to each other?* Santana was only thirteen years old.

So, he figured or assumed Simfany was the connection. He was lost and he needed answers to a lot of questions. The last time he went to question Simfany, she asked him to leave yet again. His partner Lawson insisted they send a female in to talk to Simfany, but Ramos was against it. It would only waste their time; he knew Simfany would talk to no one, no matter the gender. Snitching is snitching; he knew the code of the streets all too well. And in Simfany's world, that was not acceptable. Ramos sat back in his chair and rubbed his chin while he looked at his computer monitor. "It'll come ... it'll come," he said in a low tone to himself.

***

Justice pondered on whether or not he should get involved with the mess Baltimore had. Simfany was like his second mother, and Santana was like his brother. Being thirteen years old had its advantages but also its disadvantages. Justice was definitely willing to ride for his family, but the thought of dying in the process had him second guessing how he lived.

Justice didn't feel right just leaving Simfany in a fucked-up state. She needed him, whether he knew it or not. Justice needed to talk to his mother about the trip to Baltimore. It was one of the disadvantages of being a child. Lonnie came through the door, singing to whatever she was listening to in her headphones. She paid no attention to Justice as she walked past him. Lonnie was in the zone. He laughed at his mother as she danced salsa through the small apartment.

"Ma!" Justice called loudly, trying to grab his mother's attention. She obviously didn't hear him because she continued to salsa through the kitchen. "Ma!" he yelled this time as he waved his hands, he got her attention. Lonnie stopped dancing and took the headphones from around her ears.

"What's up, papi?" Lonnie asked.

"Ma, you know Simfany got shot and Santana is locked up, right?"

"Yeah, I know about both of them. Damn shame, she got shot. Momma tried to move away from the bullshit, yet she still got caught up in the lore of the streets. I just talked to her about a week ago. She is no longer in ICU. Why, what's wrong?" She could see the stress in her son's face. Justice let the anger subside, his mother knew about what happened and didn't tell him.

"I think Simf need us more than ever right now. We really the only family she has that really cares about her. At least, can I go out there to help her for a while? I know school but understand, she would do it for you. Santana would also do the same for you, I hope. Nah, fuck that, I know he would. So, think about that." Lonnie thought about what Justice said and by all means what he was saying made sense, but what the fuck did she look like sending her thirteen-year-old son out to another city. *Yeah right!* she thought quickly.

"Baby, I love Simfany as much as you do, if not more. That's been my bitch since the sandbox. But you're my main priority. Nigga, if you were to go out there and fuck around and get hurt, I wouldn't be able to forgive myself," she explained as she leaned against the refrigerator. She looked him in his eyes for what seemed like an eternity. What scared her most was she saw no spark left behind his eyes. The sparkle that was there was now a dim light.

The last past eight months would be rough on any child, even one growing up in the belly of the beast. His cousin was shot in his face, his best friend moved, leaving only Peewee and he was seldomly around. And to sum it all up, his godmother was laid in a hospital bed with six bullet holes in her body. That would guarantee to fuck with any child. Justice never talked about the situations that transpired so she never spoke on it or even thought about it. but as she stared into his eyes, she began to understand. Tears rolled down Lonnie's face. Justice got up and wiped away his mother's tears.

Justice didn't understand why the emotional change, but whatever it was he reached out and hugged her. He loved his mother more than anything.

"I love you, Ma. Simfany shouldn't have to be going through this shit," he said as he shed his own tears. "Please let me go to Baltimore for Simfany. She needs me, Ma." He looked up. Again, Lonnie saw no innocence left in her son.

"I'm sorry, papi, but I can't. Not my only son. I can't live without you in my life, Justice." Lonnie meant her every word.

"Ight Ma, but remember, she wouldn't do you like that." Regardless, she stuck to her guns.

"But papi, I can't." She began to cry uncontrollably. She knew that telling him no hurt both of them equally. Justice, because he couldn't be loyal to the people he called his family. Lonnie, because she couldn't let him go be loyal to the people she loved the most. It was a fucked-up situation, but it wasn't much she could do but be a mother. She would lay her life down for Simfany singlehandedly, but by no means would she let her son be so stupid.

"I know how much you love them, but losing you is a chance I'm not willing to take," she finalized as she wiped her tears away.

"I understand and I respect your judgment. I just hope it ain't the wrong decision," Justice said as he left the kitchen. Lonnie stayed in the kitchen and cried her eyes out over the stress and misery Simfany was probably going through. Justice really couldn't understand, but she knew what was best for him. Lonnie wiped her eyes and smiled at the loyalty Justice possessed for Simfany and Santana. Lonnie knew eventually that would be the reason for her son's demise. If Lonnie only knew ...

***

Simfany was finally released from the hospital. It felt like a thousand pounds was lifted off of her shoulders. She was still sore as hell, but she toughed it out. Every step was excruciating.

The bullets didn't necessarily burn; the aftereffect was the most painful part of her ordeal. This was a feeling Simfany wanted no parts of. *This street shit is done for me,* she said to herself. Her life and her son's life meant more than the bullshit she was wrapped up in. *That's what I live for, right? To be the best mother and live my life.*

All those thoughts ran through her head as she waited on her hack, otherwise known as a cab, to come and get her. She was on her way outside of the city Harford County was her next step. She hoped Edmondson Avenue would be the last block she would ever step foot on again. As the hack pulled up, the doctor assisted her into the vehicle. It was a struggle for Simfany to get into the cab because of her injuries, but with the help of the doctor, Simfany made it inside without incident.

"Where to, shorty?" the hack man asked.

"Take me to the county please. You know where Harford County is?" she asked.

"Yeah shorty, what part? Where do you need to go?" he asked looking at her through his rearview mirror. She opened her purse and looked at the paper she held in her hand.

"Take me to Havre de Grace, I think this say HillTop Projects," she replied, putting the piece of paper back into her bag.

"Say no more, shorty, sit back and relax. We'll be there in like forty-five minutes." He put the car into drive and pulled away from the hospital. Simfany did exactly what the hack man advised, she sat back and relaxed. With all that was going on, she didn't understand what kind of situation she was getting herself into again by moving to the county. Harford County was where all of Byrd's goons resided. If they thought she played a part in Byrd's death, all hell would break loose. She was naive to the fact of the harm she would be putting herself in.

***

Justice was feeling what his mother was talking about, but deep inside he knew she knew what was best for him. Bogus would probably be mad about the outcome of her decision, but it was what it would be. Va-Holla as a whole would have to understand. He hoped they would at least. He picked up the phone and dialed his mentor's number. As the phone rang, his thoughts ran wild, he didn't want to look weak to his niggas.

"Hello?" a strong baritone voice answered the phone.

"Bogus, I need to see you whenever you get the time."

"Where you at? I'm in Melrose right now. You in the hood?"

"Yeah."

"Little nigga, this shit important?" Bogus asked impatiently.

"Very."

"Ight, I'm in apartment 3A."

"What building, 681?" Justice asked.

"Yeah, slide through soon. I'll be waiting on you." Justice started to think twice about telling Bogus he wasn't going to Baltimore. All that remained in his head was that he was thirteen years old at the end of the day. He understood where he was raised and what he saw on a daily basis, but no child should be exposed to that and forced to grow into a man that fast. His mother was right, and it began to dawn on him that he wasn't about to get smoked that easily.

Justice walked to 681. As he reached apartment 3A, he stopped and tried to regain his composure. When he leveled his breathing, he knocked on the door. No one answered. When Justice went to knock again, the door behind him opened.

"Come on, son," Bogus called from inside the doorway. *Am I trippin' or did this nigga say 3A?* he thought as he made his way into the apartment. Bogus closed the door and walked into the kitchen. Justice followed behind him without question. It looked like a bakery inside the kitchen.

"Grab a chair and tell me what's on your mind," Bogus stated as he turned down the pot of boiling water. Justice sat in the first chair closest to Bogus.

"I'm gone keep it all the way real with you, helping Simfany is out of the question. Not because I don't love my lady, but because my mother said her piece on the situation." He looked at Bogus for a sign of disapproval, but he remained expressionless. Justice continued. "First off, my mom's not gone let me go. You must understand, I'm thirteen, son. This not the mafia, niggas not just running around clapping and killing shit. That's my familia we talking about, but some things must be handled at a different angle. That angle just not me right now. My mother doesn't want to bury me and truthfully, I don't want to be buried," Justice explained.

"I do understand, son, but your second guessing got me wondering about your loyalty to Va-Holla. You keep talking about this age shit. That doesn't mean anything. That metal makes you a man, son. Word to my mother, you acting sleazy, my G." Bogus shook his head. "On some real shit, what potential do you have if you play, you play by the rules? Loyalty

For the Love of Blood

being one, shit, loyalty being the only one," he concluded. Justice laughed at what he said, because in all reality he was right, loyalty was number one.

"What you giggling like a bitch for? Your G on trial right now, bro." Bogus got mad.

"With all due respect, my nigga, I may be young but I'm not stupid by any meaning of the word, and I realized something thanks to you, *big homie*. Loyalty is number one and yet I gave it all to Va-Holla, while my mother came in last place every time. So, to do us both a favor, I won't mention Va-Holla again. I'm good, my nigga. I'll help my familia when the time is right, Simfany and Santana know what it is with me," Justice said as he got up to leave. Bogus walked up behind Justice, grabbing his arm roughly. He looked at Justice in his eyes for a second, then let his arm go.

"Be safe, little bro, Take care of your moms. But you know if I see you mixed up in this street shit at any time, you will become the next mission. Justice, don't become a plate. This ya way out. Take it. This shit not for you." Bogus walked back into the kitchen while Justice exited the apartment. The turn of a new leaf... or was it? Justice didn't know, all he knew was Va-Holla, but Va-Holla was his past now. It hurt his heart, but it seemed as though it was the best decision to make, if not for him alone, at least for his mother. *Fuck it, it is what it is.* He told himself as he rode the three floors to the lobby. He knew he was dolo now and had nobody riding with him, besides Peewee and he was okay with that. Like he said many times before, *it is what it is.*

***

As the months went by, Simfany got settled in with her friend Carol in Havre de Grace, while Santana did dead time until his trial in December. Justice stayed away from the bullshit that the block had to offer. His mother was his number-one love and everything he did, he did it for her. As the summer turned into fall, and fall began approaching winter, niggas everywhere had plans to set shit on fire like it was the middle of the summer.

Chapter 8

Winter was near and November was almost gone. Santana was only two weeks away from his trial date, the fight of his life. Rick Holliver, the best criminal defense attorney in Baltimore was on his way to talk a plea deal with Santana. Pretty Ricky also told him he most likely would like the plea agreement, but he warned him not to sweat it. *Don't sweat it, it was only his life on the line.* He told Rick the same thing the last time they talked. Santana had knots in his stomach as he paced back and forth through the dayroom in Clinton Hall.

So many thoughts ran through his head regarding this new plea. He stopped pacing and sat down and looked out the gated window. It was a remembrance of the bad choices niggas made. Santana was nervous, he tried to go lay down, but it was another feeble attempt. Nothing seemed to help relieve his mind. His worst fear was that he would never make it home. His thoughts made his whole situation more and more difficult as the minutes passed.

Blair hadn't shown his face much lately because of the issues he and Tijuana were having, Drew was out at court seeing what his own fate would be. So, at the moment he was dolo. Santana had no one to talk to about his own issues. Tijuana had the week off due to some kind of new training that was mandatory. It was cool though. He was always alone with his thoughts anyway.

He began to pace again, waiting in his name to be called for his attorney visit. An hour or two went by before Santana began to get restless. It was around three o'clock, usually too late for an attorney visit. As soon as Santana went to lie down for the day, he heard his name being called from the front of the building.

"Santana Vasquez, where you at, lor homie?" C.O. Green shouted as he walked through Clinton Hall, looking for Santana. "You got an attorney visit, shorty," Green shouted again. Santana heard him clearly, he was so anxious he didn't move at all. In his mind he was moving though, but in reality, he was stuck. Santana was scared to death of what Pretty Ricky had to say. He got back off the bed and dressed in his best attire to look presentable. C.O. Green was standing at his door as he went to exit the room.

"Damn, lor nigga, I know you not deaf. You young niggas, yo, I swear. Hurry the fuck up, the van waiting on you," Green exclaimed as he walked back up front. Santana sped up to keep up with Green.

"My bad, son, I had to get dressed."

"First off, I'm not your son. Second, hurry the fuck up before they leave your dumbass up here."

"Okay *yo,*" Santana replied, being a smart ass. By then, they reached the front door of the unit. The double doors had certain keys to unlock them, so they had to wait for the doors to be opened before he could send Santana out to the transportation van. When they finally got out the door, the scenery was like that of a college campus. The transportation van was waiting at the curb for Santana. He hopped in the van and within two minutes he was making his way into the gym where on occasion visitation was held.

The only person sitting in the gym was his attorney, Rick Holliver. *This nigga got my fate in his hands and he just chilling like shit sweet,* he thought as he approached his lawyer. They greeted each other with a handshake and a nod. Santana took his seat across from Rick and waited for his lawyer to speak.

"How you been up here, Mr. Vasquez? Your mother told me to tell you she will be present on the fifth and also that she loves you dearly. Anyway, I'm not here for that. I'm here to get you to sign this plea I worked so hard to get you." He opened his folder and handed Santana a copy of his potential plea deal. Santana tried to read what was on the paper, he understood the concept of the plea, but he needed it told to him in layman's terms. *Lawyer language.* He shook his head. It was as if Rick could hear Santana's thoughts. So, he explained.

"Okay, what that says is they're willing to let you plea to a lesser charge of unlawful wounding, instead of the initial charge of attempted murder. The plea states they are willing to give you a chance to complete a six- to nine-month program, but at any time if you start to act up or get kicked out of the program, you will have juvenile life weighing over your head. Do you understand? No fuckups, Santana, standard behavior and you're out in nine months at the most. I believe you can make it," Rick said confidently. Santana sat there and listened to his lawyer explain the plea deal.

"Okay, let me get this straight. You're telling me I can be home in nine months? Before my birthday?"

"That's up to you Santana, but yes, it's a possibility." Santana smiled and shook his head. He was ecstatic about the news his lawyer just delivered. Rick Holliver even had the smile of satisfaction on his face.

"Do you think I should take it? Do you think Jimdog would testify?" Santana asked.

"To be truthful, I don't think he will, but you never know and there were other witnesses. And if he does, there is no way you can win. And if you don't win, you'll be gone for a long time. This is how I see it, take the plea and stay out of trouble, so you can get home and put all this behind you. When you're eighteen years old, this will never show up on any record. Not too many people get the chance you are getting today. Take advantage of it." Santana fell into heavy thought. *Would this nigga Jimdog break the code?* he asked himself. He knew one thing. It wasn't worth the risk of finding out. *Fuck it.* Santana put his name on the dotted line. He handed the paperwork back to his lawyer.

"Now all you have to do is stay out of trouble. I'll see you on the fifth. Please, Santana, stay out of harm's way," Rick told Santana as he put the plea agreement back into his briefcase.

"Thank you, Mr. Holliver. Tell my mother I love her and trust and believe I will stay out the way," Santana assured him, but deep down, he was never really too sure. Rick nodded as he listened to his client.

"Be safe." It was the last piece of advice Pretty Ricky gave Santana before he departed from the gym.

Rick was on his way to the courthouse to turn his client's plea in. He just hoped Santana would stick to his side of the agreement and stay out of trouble. His fate was in his own hands now. He did his job and got the best deal possible.

***

Hours later, Santana was laid out on his bed as he thought about his future. He had to admit, his plea was sweet. *Shit, all I have to do is a six- to nine-month program and I can go home.* He liked the thought of that. *Bet that, nigga.* He smiled. He sat back up. Santana didn't know if he wanted to lie down or pace around his room. He was excited. It was the best news he had heard since his incarceration. But the truth was, Santana didn't understand the gray area of his plea deal. It was a six- to nine-month program shot, but the slightest fuck-up and he might have to do juvenile life.

For the Love of Blood

All Santana understood was the six- to nine-month program that was guaranteed to him somewhere in Maryland. As Santana paced his cell, he thought about all that he was missing out in the real world. At the age of thirteen and in his predicament, his mind was on all the wrong things. He had court in the next two weeks and yet he paced about, thinking about Skate Key and what his friends were doing for Christmas vacation.

What was most important were the thoughts of his mother. He smiled at the thought of being home with her soon. *I gotta tell her this news.* Santana combed his hair and put it in a ponytail before he made his way up the hall to call his mother. Santana dialed his mother's last known number. He waited as the operator told him to hold or the party to answer. Santana was anxious and he didn't know why.

He got no answer, so he called back. The operator repeated the same process. This time, the phone was answered on the second ring. Santana waited again as the operator explained about the charges and the monitoring of the call. The call was connected seconds later, as the party on the other end pressed the number to connect the call.

"Hey, baby boy, how you holding up?" Simfany asked. Santana could hear her smile coming through the phone.

"Nah, how have you been, pretty lady?" He was still concerned about her condition.

"Livable, still walking around slightly slumped, my chest still broken up from the surgery. But Momma is okay, baby. I promise." Santana hated his mother going through her current turmoil. It angered him deeply. A tear ran down his face, lost in thought, he sat on the phone and said nothing.

"Helloooooo... Santana?" Simfany called out through the phone.

"Shit. My bad, Ma, I zoned out for a second. This shit will do it to you."

"First off, little nigga, watch your mouth when you're talking to me. I understand, nigga, but have some respect." Santana laughed. His mother was still spunky as hell.

"What's so funny? Boy, you're crazy." She laughed. She could hear the smile Santana held through the phone.

"Nothing, Ma. Anyway, the real reason I called is because I saw Pretty Ricky today. This nigga slid through with this beautiful ass plea deal. They want me to plead to unlawful wounding, and I will get a six- to nine-month program."

"Okay, what else?" Simfany asked.

"What do you mean what else, that's the whole plea."

"It's got to be more to it than that. You can't just run around trying to kill people and get six- to nine-month programs."

"It had some shit to do with juvenile life."

"And what the fuck did he say about that?" Simfany was curious. She knew a little of the plea, but she didn't know much.

"Kids that stay locked up until the age of twenty-one."

"Santana, what did it say?"

"That if I can't stay out of trouble to complete whatever program they give me, juvenile life hangs over my head. But that we don't have to worry about."

"I understand, Santana, but always protect yourself. I know how it can get in those places. If it's not a serious situation, stay your high yellow ass out of the way." He laughed. "Nigga, you think I'm playing with you? On a serious note, I need you home with me." Simfany began to cry.

"No reason for that, Ma. I'll be home soon," he reassured her.

"Alright, Santana, be safe. I love you and I'll be there on the fifth."

"I love you too, pretty lady. Don't worry, I'll be home this summer."

"Bye, baby."

"Alright, beautiful." Simfany hung the phone up, leaving Santana at the phone shaking his head. He hated to hear his mother stressed. If he only knew the guilt she held on a daily basis, he would understand her pain better.

Despite the phone call, Santana felt good. He hung up the phone and made his way back to his room. He had to write Justice and Marissa and tell them about his current plea. When he got into his room, he looked for paper and pen. Upon finding it, he laid down on his bed and began to write Justice first. As he was writing the first letter, he felt a presence in the room and looked up to see a figure standing in the doorway of his cell. It was Tijuana.

"What's got your nappy headed ass so happy?" Tijuana asked, showing off her pearly whites. It was the first time Santana actually took notice of how beautiful Tijuana truly was. She resembled Charli Baltimore, only brown skinned. Her smile was· one of her best attributes.

Tijuana had beautiful teeth, with two gold fronts in her canine teeth, it only added to her sex appeal. Her body was that of a goddess, standing at five-eight. He licked his lips and stood up.

"What are you doing here? I thought you were at training all this week," he asked as he hugged her.

"I did. But I didn't have shit to do so I came in, had to check on my lor souljah. Is that okay with you, daddy?"

"I guess. But let me ask a question. Why do you say lor instead of lil'?" Tijuana shrugged her shoulders.

"That's how I've been saying it since a lor girl," she answered.

"My lawyer just came, and I signed a mean ass plea deal, or at least it was a good enough plea. I pled out to a six- to nine-month program. Juvie life hangs over my head if I fuck up. As soon as I get out this bitch, I should be good." Santana leaned against the wall and held eye contact with Tijuana.

"That's what's up. Just don't go around telling all these hating ass niggas your business. They'll make sure they help you fuck it up. These lor niggas be hating on that type of luck, believe that. So, I beg you, keep ya plea deal to yourself." Santana could tell she was worried about something else. *She needed someone to talk to, that's why she came in today, h*e thought as he watched her.

"Ma, what's on your mind? I can see something's wrong. It's written all over your face. Let me know what's up," he said, still maintaining eye contact.

"I'm pregnant," Tijuana said as she wiped the tears as they fell from her eyes.

"Why do I have the feeling this is a bad thing?"

"It is. I don't want to have a baby by that nigga, Santana!"

"You're talking about Blair, right? Why not, I thought that was your boo. Okay, now I'm confused." His look told her just that.

"Nothing to be confused about, I'm not having that nigga's seed. Only if you knew, baby boy." She stood there looking into space for the right words to explain. She continued. "Your loyalty lies with that nigga, and I understand, so please leave it where it may be."

She turned to leave, but of course Santana grabbed ahold of her so she couldn't.

"What are you talking about, ma? My loyalty lies with both of y'all. Fuck all that my 'loyalty lies with him' shit. Tell me what's on ya mind. Your secrets are safe with me, I promise that," Santana said, hoping he wouldn't have to break that promise. He watched as the tears flowed down her face. Tijuana was a beautiful girl and being a correctional officer wasn't her calling, that was for sure. He leaned his back against the wall and waited. He hoped she would elaborate. Tijuana walked back into Santana's room and sat on his bed. She looked out the dirty window in silence. Santana continued to look at the woman before him, trying to unfold what secret she held inside. He spoke first.

"Ma, that's crazy you don't trust me. I have been through way too much fucking with you, for you to be acting like this. What was the point of you coming in today? It wasn't because you were bored. Beautiful, I don't mean to be mean, please forgive me, but you're really making me feel some type of way. This shit crazy." Santana started to pace his cell. But still no words came from Tijuana, she sat in silence.

"Santana ... you know I love you dearly, so I'm going to keep it real with you. I regret fucking with that nigga. I told the biggest secret I have, nothing more to tell for real. I just can't keep this boy's baby. I'll never have a baby by a nigga of his caliber, he is way too selfish. It's a lost cause, and truth be told, it's for reasons unknown. He just lame. The only reason I still mess with that lor boy is because of you. He keeps these Baltimore niggas off your back. And at times, I think it's only because of my word, that he even does that. You know, Jimdog was his man for real.

"I don't know, the nigga may really fuck with you, but I don't have time to find out what type shit he would be on, if I wasn't in the picture. You feel me? The type is an opportunist, just watch him and you'll see all signs. That's one reason I won't bear his child. Not in this fucking lifetime. So, be careful and understand most these lor nigga have ulterior motives that benefit only them." Tijuana's face lightened, she finally smiled. "Come here, Tana, and give me a hug."

She got off the bed and walked towards him. He embraced her. She rested her cheek on the top of his head as she hugged him.

"Santana, I fucks with you hard body, lor yo, and I see the potential. So always keep it real with me, and forever I'll ride with you until the wheels fall off," she whispered in his ear. She let him go and held him at arm's length as Santana's face got red. Tijuana smiled.

"I fuck wit you too, ma, more than you can imagine. Always know your secrets are safe with me." Santana didn't know what to think about Blair Mebane anymore. Maybe Tijuana was right, and his intentions were all wrong from the beginning. Santana started to believe her theory.

Why would she lie? No need to, he asked himself after Tijuana exited his room. *Fuck that bitch nigga and his man Jimdog.* Santana made a mental note to watch Blair from that day forward.

Santana just hoped he wasn't making a mistake by trusting Tijuana. He was stuck in the middle of some bullshit and his thoughts were scrambled. In due time, actions would play out and lines would be drawn between two frenemies.

***

Simfany got tired of being under Carol all day, so she set out to look for her own spot. She went apartment shopping in Havre de Grace and Aberdeen, but she didn't like the places or neighborhoods. She heard about some complexes in the Edgewood section of the county. Out of all, it was rumored to be the calmest part of the county. Simfany didn't care, she just needed a place to call her home.

For the Love of Blood

The first place she filled out an application for was a complex by the name of *Harford Square*. It was a sector with row houses sprinkled within a circled community. At first glance, it was a very beautiful place to reside, but inside of the townhouses, the rooming was way too small. It really didn't matter though, so she kept the complex in mind. She looked at a couple more places before she gave up.

The second place she filled her application out was for a complex by the name of *Windsor Valley*. The complex was huge. The inside was also beautiful and spacious. Windsor Valley was a better place for her. At the end of the day, she wanted to get out of Carol's house so whoever called first, she would be cool with. The truth was, Simfany wouldn't feel completely safe until Santana came home. It ate at Simfany's soul to know she was the cause of all the drama happening in Baltimore. The choices she made came back to haunt her son.

If I only knew who killed Byrd and why, I wouldn't be going through this fucking drama, she thought. Simfany had a lot of love for Byrd, but he wasn't worth all the drama that was brought into her life. Her son's life was the most important thing to her and by all means, she would protect him till her dying day. Each day, her thoughts of the whole situation haunted her.

***

The day finally came for Santana to go to court. He was awakened at six am that morning, awaiting transportation to the Mitchell Courthouse in downtown Baltimore. Santana didn't leave Hickey until a quarter past eight. The view from Baltimore County to the city was a luxury. Seeing any signs of life was a plus. The littlest things pegged his interest now, like stores and newsstands. The inner city was beautiful and had a lot of life. But of course, that was from the outside looking in. Santana could see the murder capital under all of the nicely built townhouses and skyscrapers.

Every block they passed had a blue light hanging at the top of its light poles. The blue lights were an indication of the cameras placed there to monitor the drug and gang activity. The mayor ordered for the cameras to be put in place, due to the outlandish murder rate that seemed to rise each year. The sad part was the cameras made no difference whatsoever. The murders were still committed, just now only recorded on camera. For better words, it wasted taxpayer's money. No matter what went on at night on the streets of Baltimore, Santana loved the sightseeing part of his trip. Santana gazed out the caged window as the buildings began to get taller and taller in downtown Baltimore. It was Charm City at its best.

The van came to a slow halt indicating the arrival at the courthouse. Santana was back to being nervous again. Even though he knew what awaited him, he still was scared to death. *What if they don't accept the plea deal?* he thought. He tried his best to eliminate all the bad thoughts he had in his head. As he hopped out of the transport van, he held his head high and walked toward the entrance of the building with confidence. The transporting officer that was escorting him spoke.

"Good luck in there today, lor man, hopefully they don't try to hang you by your feet."

"Thank you, I need it. I took a plea already, but that don't mean they can't show out on me."

"I hope that plea is a good thing. But still, I wish you the best. You will need it fucking with these white folks."

"I know that's right." Santana laughed at the old head as they stood and waited for the elevator to come.

Upon arriving upstairs, Santana was put into the bullpen, awaiting his turn in court. Unlike the other time he was there,

For the Love of Blood

other people were present. Most of the inmates were from Boys Village, a juvenile facility located in Upper Marlboro, Maryland. They mostly housed inmates from the D.C. area and the surrounding counties. Santana had a lot on his mind, so he tried not to pay the other people any mind, but one boy caught his attention. He looked to be about Santana's age, the only difference between the two was Santana's hair, and the other boy had a lot of tattoos. The look in the boy's eyes showed misery and anger. To the human eye, he looked dangerous. He looked as if he had been through a lot in life. Santana caught himself staring at the kid, but he didn't understand why. Deep down, he knew why, he didn't want to look that bitter ever in life. The other kid looked up and made eye contact with Santana.

"What's good, dog? You got an issue, shorty?" the light-skinned kid asked.

"Nah my nigga it ain't even like that, son. I was looking at the work you got on you. No harm intended, my nigga," Santana replied. Subconsciously, the boy looked at his own tattoos.

"I can feel that. What's your name, lor yo?"

"Santana," he said proudly.

"Ooooo, so you the lor nigga that popped that bitch ass nigga Jimdog?" the boy laughed.

"If that's what you wanna call it," Santana replied, wondering how his name was still associated with the shooting.

"I wish you would have smoked that pussy, for real. The lor nigga run around over East playing tough like he built like that. Shorty ain't even like that. I personally wouldn't miss him, you feel me?"

"I can feel that. I really didn't know son like that. I was just put in a situation to protect my raise, my G." Santana continued. "What's your name, my G?"

"They call me Johnny Man in my hood."

"No disrespect, but you look young, son. How old are you?" Santana asked curiously.

Johnny Man laughed.

"No disrespect taken. I'm only fourteen, shorty, I been through hell though, shorty. Shit, my nigga, I been through too much for real. In order to survive in Body More, Murdaland, you have to grow up fast or get found in the field. I refuse to be found floating in the harbor, shorty. I'm not with the early graves."

"I can understand that. What you booked for?"

"Damn, lor yo, you ask a lot of questions. But you cool. I'm already booked for a controlled substance. They got me in court today because me and my man banked this lor C.O. nigga in Hickey a while back. We broke shorty's face, so they charged us with the assault. I beat the charges in the county, but you know these white folks find some kind of way to smash a nigga in the end. They sent my man to Townsend because he was already sixteen when we caught the charges, so they waived him up. Ain't shit though, what's the ironic part about the situation is we thrashed a D.C. staff member, so they sent me to where all his family works. Crazy, huh?"

Johnny Man shrugged it off and Santana could tell he really didn't care. It didn't seem to bother him in the least.

"Santana Vasquez, get ready for court, you're up next," Bailiff Lawrence called out.

"Okay," Santana replied. He looked over at Johnny Man and nodded. "Pleasure to meet you, my G, continue to hold it down," Santana stated as he rose and waited at the gate for the bailiff.

"Ight, lor yo. You make sure you do the same. Keep in touch, shorty. My real name is Johnny Ariza. Yo know where

For the Love of Blood

I'm at, lor yo. And all I do is keep it G, shorty, but I do appreciate the advice," Johnny Man replied. Pretty Ricky appeared only moments later, with the bailiff in tow. Before Santana left, he looked back and nodded his silent goodbye.

"Ight, lor yo," was the last thing Johnny Man said as he made his way out the bullpen and down the hall to the packed courtroom.

Santana entered the courtroom and instinctively looked around to see who all was in the courtroom. As he surveyed the room, he made eye contact with his mother. Simfany waved. Santana was happy to see his mother in attendance and out of the hospital. He continued his walk but came to a halt when he locked eyes with Jimdog. The look Santana gave Jimdog sent chills down Simfany's body. Simfany knew all too well what the meaning of the look meant. She just hoped Santana wouldn't turn into one of them kind of niggas. A killer.

"Fuck you looking at, bitch ass nigga?" Santana said, hatred bellowing through his tone. They say if looks could kill Jimdog would have been dead, in this case that was an understatement. Death was the one way the beef between them would end.

"I know ... I know ... I got you, dog. I'm going to bury your mother, you lor bitch," Jimdog replied with a smirk on his face. Without hesitation, Santana rushed Jimdog. Jimmy stood up and waited for Santana to come close enough so he could sleep him, but Santana never made it because his steps were cut short when the bailiff stepped on Santana's shackle chain, sending him to the ground in pain.

"Ahhhhhhhh," Santana screamed out, the pain that shot through his body was crazy.

"You's a bitch nigga. I'ma kill you, pussy, I swear to God!" Santana wouldn't stop spazzing. Simfany ran over to him and tried to calm him down.

"Baby, please calm down. That nigga can't hurt me, he in hiding himself. I'm good. Carlos out for that nigga's head, so please calm down. I love you, baby boy. Calm down, please." Simfany bent down and kissed Santana on the cheek. Her *kiss* calmed Santana down almost instantly. Pretty Ricky and Bailiff Lawrence helped Santana up back to his feet.

"Listen, Mr. Vasquez, I understand the emotion behind this case, but if you ever come in my courtroom and do some shit like that again... " The bailiff leaned in closer and finished his sentence. "I will fuck you up myself. Do you understand?"

"Whatever, nigga," Santana said through clenched teeth. They picked Santana up and walked him over to the defense table. He took his seat, still furious. Pretty Ricky sat his paperwork pertaining to Santana's case on the table. The judge hadn't come out of her chambers yet, thankfully. So, Santana was left alone with his thoughts and his lawyer's aggravation. "Who the fuck is Carlos?" he continued to ask himself.

"Excuse me?" Pretty Ricky asked as he turned and faced Santana.

"Oh, nothing, just thinking out loud." Rick went back to his task at hand. Santana made a mental note to check into this Carlos nigga his mother spoke of.

"All rise, court is now in session," Bailiff Lawrence announced as Judge Price came through the door. Judge Price took her seat and looked through the papers placed on her desk for the day's activities.

"You may be seated," Bailiff Lawrence said, almost robot-like.

"Okay, docket number 02-K-252, State v. Vasquez. As I understand, Mr. Vasquez signed a plea agreement. Am I right, Mr. Holliver?" she asked as she looked up toward the defense table.

Rick Holliver stood and replied. "Yes, Your Honor. That is correct."

"Thank you, Mr. Holliver. Does the prosecution have anything for me?" Judge Price waited. DA Walker stood.

"No, Your Honor, we don't have anything at this time. We agree to the facts of the plea that Mr. Vasquez signed," Mrs. Walker answered before she sat down.

"Okay. Thank you. Mr. Vasquez, I want you to understand there is no room for error. I'll expect you to follow the terms of this plea to a T. And if you ever pull a stunt like you just did in my courtroom again, there will be a steep consequence. Let's just say I advise you not to come back in front of me again. I pray I don't see you anymore after you are freed. With that, Mr. Vasquez, I wish you the best. Next case, Mr. Lawrence. Docket number 01..."

Santana turned and looked back in search of his mother. Simfany was on her way out the door when they made eye contact. Simfany blew him a kiss and mouthed, "I love you." Santana understood why his mother was in such a hurry to leave, plus he knew Mr. Lawrence wouldn't be as generous as the last time, because of the situation with Jimdog only minutes earlier. He was cool with that.

Santana loved his mother so much, it killed him that she was keeping secrets from him. Of course, he would always love his mother, but the secrets had him feeling some type of way. There was a lot that needed to be discussed between the two.

As he was driven back to Hickey, he sat and thought about the plea deal he just was granted. He thought about his mother and the whole situation regarding his incarceration. No matter what he thought about, he couldn't get the name *Carlos* out of his head. He had no idea who the name belonged to and why

Jamel Mitchell

Jimdog was hiding from him, but he promised himself he would find out.

Chapter 9

Santana was awakened by something burning and the C.O.s yelling for everybody to exit the building. Santana didn't understand what the emergency was, so he took his time. To smell smoke or something burning on Clinton Hall was common. It was a set of niggas from Chapel Hill that kept cigarettes and weed on deck, so the power sockets were popped on a regular basis. New inmates didn't have a clue on what they were doing, so most of the time the pod remained smoky. Whenever he smelled burnt paper, he didn't react to it.

"Nigga, get the fuck up! Hurry up!" Green yelled through the doorway. Santana wiped the cold out his eye and got up to see what was going on. He poked his head out the door and looked down the hall. The smoke was too thick to see the end of the hall, flames were literally shooting out a room at the end of the hall. It was crazy how the flames danced against the walls.

"Oh shit!" Santana said. He rushed back into his room and grabbed everything that had any value or meaning to him. Outside stood close to forty inmates. Some looked concerned, but the majority didn't care. They actually found it amusing. Santana stood in the middle. He didn't care about the fire, but at the same time, he wouldn't wish that kind of pain on any of the people in attendance. As all the staff filed out the building, they brought out one last inmate. He was covered in soot, so it was obvious he was the person that set the fire, it looked as if it was done purposely. Everyone stared at the boy covered in black. Santana shook his head. *Niggas always do the dumbest shit,* he thought.

"Fuck you niggas looking at? Any of you swine ass niggas got an issue, you already... " His words were cut short as a dark-skinned kid swung, connecting with his jaw. They banged, nobody jumped in or attempted to break up the fight. They fought until neither had anything left to give. The staff found it amusing, they watched also. That was a norm anyway at the Hickey School, if you had an issue, it was impossible to dodge rec. You had to fight. When the two decided the fight was over, everybody was told to line up, by height.

Nobody moved.

"What the fuck you niggas waiting on? Line the fuck up! I gotta find out where you stupid niggas going to live at until this shit cleaned up. So right now, the gym is your new home."

"Dog you ain't gotta talk to us like that. For real, you ain't bout shit, you swine ass nigga," Blair stated.

"Say no more, lor yo. But know this, you will line up today." C.O. Green stepped closer, showing he wasn't afraid of the challenge.

"Yeah, I know that's right, dog." Blair smiled. Tijuana watched quietly in disgust. She began to realize what kind of nigga she had been fucking with. After the standoff between the two, Santana stepped to the curb to form the line. He was the smallest in the pod, so he was most likely always first, Blair being the tallest, he was last. C.O. Stone took the back, Green commanded the middle of the line, and Tijuana played the front of course, next to Santana. They wanted to keep Blair and Green as far away from each other as possible.

Santana led everyone to the dining hall to eat breakfast. The two that had fought in front of the pod were taken to medical for treatment, then the hole for a cool-down period. The kid who supposedly started the fire, his name was Edmonds, he was from Park Heights. After they finished eating, they were escorted to the gym. The gym was located next to the medical center. All forty inmates in the gym were awaiting housing. Some played basketball, while others played cards.

For the Love of Blood

What caught Santana's attention was the look plastered on Blair's face. He seemed stuck in one place. Santana followed his gaze just to see what held his attention so boldly. Santana instantly began to laugh out of habit, but in all reality, it was funny about what they might assume was taking place. Tijuana was so caught up in flirting with C.O. Green, she wasn't aware of the attention she was generating.

Santana shook his head, he had a lot of love for Tijuana, but at times, she played the game wrong. He made a mental note to check her. He sat back and just observed Blair from afar, knowing in his mind that shit had the potential to get ugly.

Out of the corner of his eye, he saw Tijuana walk off to leave the building. He saw the chance, so he got up and ran trying to catch up to her. They had to talk because she was trippin'.

"Yo, ma, hold up!" Santana yelled after her. As he caught up to her, he felt holes being burnt into his back. Off instinct he turned around, but no one was paying him any attention. He searched the gym for Blair, Blair had moved from the stage. Santana got kind of nervous; he knew his man was mad over the flirting games between Tijuana and Green. He wasn't trying to be the butt of the beef. He stopped and surveyed the whole gym again, looking for Blair. When his eyes caught sight of Blair, he was in a heated conversation with C.O. Green. What he found weird was, the conversation was in hushed tones. He watched as Blair shook his head and walked off, going to his original spot in the gym, the stage.

Santana turned to holla at Tijuana.

"What's up, baby boy?" she asked with a Kool-Aid smile on her face.

"What you all smiles for? Anyway, it doesn't matter. You still fuck with the nigga Blair, right?"

"First off, I'm happy because I enjoy life. Secondly... no, I don't fuck with that bitter ass nigga anymore. Well, technically yeah, but emotionally nah. I told you what it was. It's all for *you,* Santana." She laughed seductively. She was high off life that was for sure. She continued. "And before you ask, no, I don't fuck with the lor nigga Green. Can a girl have fun sometimes?" She shrugged.

"I can't be mad at you, ma, you're grown. Real nigga shit though, ma, stop playing with that boy's emotions. And don't feel like you have to hold on for me, I'm good. I can go just as hard as the rest of these Baltimore niggas. Age doesn't matter, ma, I got heart. Win, lose or draw, I'm good. So, live your life, *baby girl.* Always know I fucks with you, hard body. I rather see you happy for real than you play house with a nigga you not feeling.

"If he only fuck with me on the strength of you then fuck him, so be it. We'll get to cross that bridge when we get there. Do you. The cards are going to played how they're meant to be played. Only time will tell. I'm good, ma, take my word for it, but please stop dragging the nigga along." Santana looked Tijuana in her eyes to show the severity of the game she was playing.

"Don't worry, baby boy, whatever I do here is for *us.* Yeah, I said *us,* lor nigga. So, you let me play the cards how I see fit. Can you do that for me?" she asked and he nodded.

"It's your world. Stop calling me, baby boy, that's what my moms calls me. Plus, it ain't shit little about me, but my feet and my height. No disrespect." They both busted out laughing.

"None taken, got that one, shorty," Tijuana replied as she walked out the gym. Santana watched her strut out the door. *Damn, that's a bad bitch.* He walked back into the gym and sat down on the stage waiting for lunch to be called.

For the Love of Blood

The day began to wind down. It was about an hour before shift change, when everybody heard a commotion coming from the bathroom area of the gymnasium. Nobody ran to the noise. Everyone knew the familiar noise all too well. Someone was in the bathroom fighting. *Lock-in's* as they were called in Baltimore. Santana surveyed the crowd to see what two were missing. Nobody of any importance was missing, so he tried to pay no mind to it, but only seconds after that thought, it hit him.

"Oh shit," he whispered to himself. He looked for Blair and Green. He looked for Tijuana also, she was in the middle of a spades game with Drew, C.O. Stone and some new light-skinned cat named Oz. None of them seemed hip to the fight or for better words, they didn't care. The scuffing of sneakers came to a halt, the thumping did also. The fight was over. Every inmate in the gym looked over towards the bathroom to see who would come out first. Green came back into the gym wiping blood from his face, walked over to the card table and got his cards back from Oz. Blair came out of the bathroom, even from a far distance you could see the left side of his face was swollen, black and purple.

He also had various speed knots sporadically around his face. Chatter began all around the gym. How Santana saw it, you win some and you lose some. Santana got his ass whooped often when he first came, so he adopted that motto fast. He wasn't a pushover though, all of Hickey knew that. He wasn't liked much, but he was respected. Santana got up from his seat and walked to the staggering Blair. He grabbed Blair in an attempt to help.

Blair pulled his arm away and looked Santana in his eyes, Santana saw the bitterness that laid dormant there. The look Blair gave him was that of pure hatred. The look was all he remembered before he felt the impact of a fist and fell into darkness ...

Chapter 10

"Pass the blunt, nigga, damn!" Diana called from the back seat of the Bonneville.

"Hold up, shorty, Blaze bout to come out his spot. You know he's fresh home. A blunt what that nigga needs in his life," Dre replied to his longtime girlfriend. Andre and Narvel were friends from back in the day. Blaze was coming home from doing a twelve- to eighteen-month bid at Hickey. Dre wanted to show his nigga some love, so he came through to fuck with him. The part that got most people was ... Dre and Blaze grew up on different sides of the flag. Dre was Shotgun Crip and Blaze was Tree Top Piru. They never let the color come in between the love and loyalty they had for one another.

"Ight, my bad, didn't know why we was over here." She said smartly as she continued to pout and look out the back seat window. No sooner than she said that a dark figure came from around the back of the car with his hands buried deep into his hoodie.

"Baby!" Diana called out, watching the man walk up, fear written all over her face. Before Dre could answer, the dark figure tapped on the driver's side window. *Man fuck!* Dre thought as he looked up. *I have to stop coming in these niggas hood without my muthafuckin tone on me.* It was too late to play pussy. He rolled the window down. There was nothing he could do even if he wanted to, the car was in park, and he had no strap. *You live like a goon, you gotta die like a goon.* He had that tatted on the left side of his chest; it was a motto he lived by.

"What's cracking, fam?" Dre looked up at what looked like the grim reaper.

"What's poppin', young bull?" Hood Ru asked as he pulled the hoodie off his head. Dre breathed a sigh of relief.

"Damn nigga, ya scary ass turned white, Ock." Hood laughed hysterically.

"Fuck you, nigga." Dre was pissed he let Hood Ru catch him slipping like that.

"I just came to holla at you, homie, damn. You know you good in this hood any day," Hood said, meaning every word. You couldn't tell Dre that though. *Sounds good.*

"Right… right, I feel you, cuz. The love the same over here, my nigga, you know that. What's good though? How you been living, shorty?" Dre asked, still suspicious of Hood Ru's intent.

"I wanted to thank you for looking out for the lor homie while y'all was locked up in Hickey. I know that young bull stay in his bag, half the time that lor nigga be drawn for no reason. But he told me you rode regardless. On my hood, nigga, good looking. You be safe young bull, if you need anything get at me, real wrap." Hood nodded his head at Dre and walked away, heading back to the house they were parked in front of. *This nigga Blaze better hurry up, got me out here like a sitting duck for real. What the fuck is this nigga doing?* He re-lit the blunt and took two strong pulls before he passed it to the back seat where Diana sat quietly. Diana gladly accepted the Dutch. The purp was meant for Blaze, but Dre needed to calm his nerves. He couldn't have his shorty seeing him sweat like that. As they passed the weed back and forth, Blaze finally made his way out the house. Blaze got to the car and hopped in the passenger side.

"What the fuck took you so long?" Dre asked, irritated. Blaze looked at Dre, and then he turned over the seat to give Diana a hug.

"How you doing today, shorty?" Blaze asked Diana, ignoring Dre and his attitude.

"I'm good, how you been, Narvel?"

For the Love of Blood

"Shit, you already know," he replied. Blaze turned around and looked at his best friend.

"Damn nigga, hi to you too. You know my moms be on that bullshit when I first come home. So, miss me with all that bullshit you talking. You're acting like a female. Pass the blunt." He reached out to get the blunt from Dre. Dre pulled on the blunt again.

"Bitch ass nigga," Dre said before he passed the blunt to Blaze pulling out of Harford Commons. The Commons was known as a kill zone in the county. It was a high crime and drug area. But most of all, it was known to be the home of the biggest gang the county had, Tree Top Piru.

Dre lived in the Ville, also another high drug and crime area. It was a high-rise complex located behind the Giant Supermarket off of Route 40. The Ville was considered the more dangerous of the two hoods. Bodies were dropped on a regular basis. There were two sides to the complex, with many gangs sprinkled within its walls. The most common and feared gang there was the Shotgun Crip niggas. Blue overrode everything on that side of the county. And if anybody went against it, body after body was left to rot. It was all for the love of the game.

Dre was a young nigga that had a lot of respect in his hood. At times his loyalty was questioned because of the company he kept, but he didn't allow that to interfere with how he moved. Dre pulled up the left side of the complex and parked in front of his building. The three of them just sat and talked.

"So, what's been good out here in these streets?" Blaze asked Dre.

"Same shit, same bitches and the same wack ass niggas, you ain't been missing nothing but the money, cuz." Diana gave Dre a cold stare through the rear-view mirror.

"I wasn't talking about you, Diana, so calm ya Spanish ass down. Always somewhere talking shit and taking things personal," Dre said, catching her glare through the rear view.

"Yeah... aight, puta, you better watch your mouth," Diana responded. Blaze laughed. He knew how much she hated the *bitch* word. Dre and Diana had been together since the early days of elementary school. The beginning of time as Blaze always called it, so it was normal that they argued on a constant basis.

"Fuck you laughing at, Blaze, get the fuck out my car! Both of you." He turned off the car and exited the car. Blaze and Diana looked at each other before they followed Dre out the car.

"Nigga, you do some shit like that again and I'm going to beat that ass," Blaze said, referring to Dre's last action. Without hesitation, Dre ran up on Blaze swinging, trying to get Blaze to slap box. Blaze held his hip and ran away. Dre stopped chasing Blaze because he knew that limp all too well. Blaze was strapped. He couldn't blame him though.

"There you go, cuz, on that bullshit already. You ain't get enough time for clapping those Aberdeen cats?" Dre asked in a more serious tone.

"I gotta be ready at all times, big bro. You know that, especially when I'm mobbing over here. I know niggas don't like me. Plus, y'all breed killers back here. On some trill shit, homie, I would never come back here if I wasn't fucking with you." Blaze looked around then pulled the .20 gauge sawed-off. He placed the gun behind the wheel of Dre's car. The jump outs and the gang unit lurked at all hours of the day. That Tuesday and Thursday theory was bullshit. He couldn't keep it on him, but he tried to keep it as close as possible. Dre shook his head, but he understood how Blaze might feel. He just felt that way only hours ago when he was in The Commons. Dre hated the thought of being caught slipping. He wholeheartedly understood his friend's precaution.

Dre pulled out the last bag of weed, Blaze pulled out the blunts, while Diana smiled at the thought of getting high, again. The trio sat and got baked as they reminisced about their days of innocence. They talked about the ups and downs of being locked up at Hickey. Shortly after, Diana departed, she had school in the morning. The old friends sat and talked about life in general. Blaze realized time had crept by as he looked at his phone. It was late.

"I'm trying to shoot back to the spot, homie. Hood needed me to handle something for him tonight, so drive me back to The Commons, shorty," Blaze said as he jumped off the hood of the Bonneville.

"Aight, give me a couple minutes to get my mind right." Dre slid off the car and stretched. No sooner than five minutes later, shit hit the fan.

"Crrrrrriiiiiiiiipppppp... Clatttt... Crrrrrriiiiiiiiipppppppp," was all that could be heard in the distance. He looked over at Blaze and shook his head as a sign of apology. Two dark figures appeared from out of the building next to the cut, Blaze didn't recognize none of them.

"What's crackin', cuz? I see you got this nigga out here again," the taller one of the two exclaimed.

"Chill, Kane, you know this my nigga. We held it down for the county when we were booked. I fuck with shorty hard body, cuz," Dre explained.

"Fuck that nigga. Hood and the rest of them slob ass T.T.P. niggas like to bust on sight, why should I let this bitch ass nigga walk away? Man, fuck that nigga." Blaze looked at Kane, and then he looked at the wheel of the Bonneville where the .20 gauge was hidden from plain view. Kane was too far gone to see the gesture.

"Fuck you, you crab ass bitch!" Blaze spat at both men. Blaze looked at Dre, silently telling him he meant no offense. "What's poppin', nigga, you need help? You that pussy nigga from Deen, right? Exactly, that's all y'all niggas do down there is bank muthafucka. I'd smash you on the one tip." Blaze was letting his emotions get the best of him.

"We don't fight slobs round here, cuz, we lay them niggas to rest," Kane said as he showed Blaze the butt of his gun. Blaze knew it was no way he could get to the .20 gauge without letting Kane smoke him. So, he played his cards the best way he could.

"You got that, shorty, all I want to do is leave. I won't come back over this bitch, I can promise you that," Blaze pleaded. His goal was to live and see another day.

"You hear this shit, cuz?" Kane tapped the little nigga he had with him.

"This nigga bitching up when he seen the tone wink, where your heart at now, playboy?" Kane asked, this time upping his strap.

"Chill cuz, I was about to take him home," Dre tried to assure Kane.

"I should blow both you bitches heads off." Kane slurred his words, the shorter cat that was with Kane pulled his arm down.

"Chill shorty, these niggas don't want no smoke," Ty said.

"Ty, fuck these niggas, it's just funny how muthafuckas turn pussy when they see metal," Kane expressed.

"Dre, fam… cuz, you trippin'. Them E pills got you trippin, shorty, for real. Let that nigga slide, fam. We can catch that pussy somewhere else. Do it for me, shorty?" Ty tried his best to calm Kane down. Kane listened to Ty and put his gun away hesitantly.

"See you around, cuz." Kane stared at both men and didn't indicate who he might be talking to. Blaze didn't care, he was just trying to leave.

"Come on, yo." Blaze grabbed Dre by the arm, ready to leave. Blaze saw the fire in Dre's eyes. Dre pulled out of his grasp and reached under the car for the shotgun. He grabbed the .20 gauge and walked toward Kane, calling his name.

"Kane!" Kane turned around. Without any second thought, Dre pulled the trigger, blowing a hole into Kane's body. Ty hesitated, but he tried to pull his strap. Dre didn't give him the chance he fired on him also. Dre missed. Ty had enough time to take cover behind the dumpster that sat in the middle of the complex. Ty looked from behind the dumpster to see Dre standing over Kane. Kane wasn't moving. It was no saving him so he took off, leaving his fallen comrade.

Dre looked into Kane's eyes. He was in a state of shock. He couldn't believe what he had just done. He had grown up in diapers with Kane, only for it to end like this. Over some gang shit. By all means, Dre was a soldier and did niggas dirty plenty of times, but this was his family, or so he thought.

Kane laid on the pavement struggling to breathe, gargling his own blood. Kane looked into Dre's eyes, pleading through his tears for help. Dre put all the memories and emotions aside and pulled the trigger on the sawed-off, ending Kane's life for good. Dre wiped his face and took off into a full sprint. He hopped in the car. Blaze was still shocked over Dre killing Kane, so his reaction was slow.

"Hurry up, nigga. Hop the fuck in. Fuck... Fuck... " Dre screamed. He threw the shotgun in the back seat and pulled off. Blue lights were coming in the direction Dre needed to hit the interstate, so he went the opposite way of the sirens. Dre was scared. He let his emotions get the best of him. He wasn't thinking rationally. Once the blue lights faded, they calmed down.

"Where the fuck we going?" Blaze asked.

"I don't know, fam. I'm trying to get away from here. Grab the tone and wipe the fingerprints off," Dre said, panicking. Blaze grabbed the gun and wiped it down to the best of his ability.

"You done?"

"Yeah," Blaze replied. As Dre continued to drive, he looked for a spot to dump the sawed-off. Finally satisfied, he pulled up to a house with a large bush in the yard.

"Put that bitch in there," Dre said, pointing at the bush. Blaze hesitated, but he did as he was told.

"Where you trying to go, shorty?" Dre asked Blaze.

"Anywhere close," Blaze replied.

"I'm going to drop you off in Meadowood. You out there, right?"

"Yeah." Dre drove a couple minutes, arriving at the Shell gas station. Meadowood was only a flight of stairs away from the Shell. Dre pulled over to let Blaze out.

"Look yo, my bad for getting you into this bullshit. Tell Hood to send one of those niggas to come and get you. It's a war now, so be safe out here. Them Shotgun Crip niggas going to know you ain't have nothing to do with it, because Ty was there. He gone tell all, but still, stay strapped just in case. Always know you my lor nigga and I love you, bro." Dre hugged Blaze before he pulled off. Dre made his way onto I-95 North, safely on his way to Philadelphia, Pennsylvania.

It wasn't far from Baltimore but it was far enough for the time being. Dre made his way into Philly without a problem, but meanwhile Blaze was shackled and handcuffed in the Harford County Sheriff's barracks. He was being charged with the murder of Kane Moore. Blaze had a lot of love for Dre, but

For the Love of Blood

him just being released only twenty-four hours earlier was all that crossed his mind.

Blaze didn't know what he was going to do. One thing was sure, and two things were certain, a murder bid wasn't in his cards. He sat in the interrogation room with his head against the table. He was fucked in all honesty, and he knew it.

The detective came into the room with a pen and a notepad. He sat the pad and pen in front of Blaze and said, "It's your only way out, Mr. Harris, and it's up to you to take it. We have witnesses that put the two people at the murder scene. And what I know, you don't have the attributes to be the shooter, but being there and knowing it was going to happen is just enough to get at least twenty years out of you. You better think about it, Narvel, because we finally got your ass." Just as fast as the detective came in and left out, Blaze was left in thought.

Blaze shook his head at his fate and a tear rolled down his face. Blaze died when he picked the pen up and buried the nigga who stopped him from being murdered. *Fuck that nigga, ...* was all Blaze thought as he wrote his statement. Dre had no clue the only witness they had was the man he loved like a brother. Blaze told everything he knew in hopes of getting out of trouble.

Jamel Mitchell

Chapter 11

Santana woke up in the infirmary with a bad headache. He put his hands on his head and rubbed his hands through his hair. The right side of his face was throbbing. Santana opened his eyes to see Tijuana and Drew talking to the nurse on call. *"What the fuck happened?"* he asked himself. He couldn't remember what put him in the infirmary. He began to rise, but he instantly grew lightheaded. He didn't have the chance to catch his balance before his feet slipped off the corner of the cot. Santana fell halfway off the bed before he was able to catch himself. The nurse, Tijuana and Drew watched as he struggled to get back on the cot. The nurse walked up and helped him back onto the bed. Drew laughed at his friends' clumsiness. The nurse waited for Santana to get right before she took his vitals and a small physical. She had to make sure he was okay.

"You are going to have a headache for a little while, but you'll be okay by tonight. What you need to do is stop getting into all these physical altercations. It's not good at your age. I mean that, boy," Santana smiled.

"You got it, Ms. Thomas," he replied. Ms. Thomas was a stern old lady that worked for the medical department in Hickey. Everybody hated when they had to come to medical and see her, everybody but Santana. Santana liked Ms. Thomas. He knew she was stern but cool in her own way.

"Okay, Mr. Vasquez. I will hold you to that." Santana smiled, thinking she was playing, Ms. Thomas was as serious as a heart attack. Ms. Thomas walked over to Tijuana.

"Ms. Moore, you can take these boys back whenever you're ready." Ms. Thomas grabbed Santana and Drew's folders and left the room.

"Damn, Ms. Thomas kicked us out. Y'all lor niggas ready?" Tijuana asked.

"Yup," they said simultaneously. Santana hopped off the cot and noticed Drew had a black eye also.

"Damn nigga, what happened?" Santana asked.

"Come on, shorty, I couldn't let that nigga do you like that. Win, lose or draw, remember?"

"I understand, but what happened, my G?" Santana asked him again. Drew explained what happened leading up to both of them being in the infirmary. Santana was pissed at the news he heard.

"I'ma kill that bitch ass nigga. I knew someone hit me but damn him. It's straight, I got something for that nigga."

"Calm down, baby boy. Oh, and by the way, I will make sure that boy's stay won't be so good," Tijuana said. She walked them through the infirmary to the main control center, to wait for transportation to take them back to the gym.

"T, ain't none of these Baltimore niggas gone ride against Blair," Drew said, knowing Tijuana's thought most likely wouldn't happen. She stared at him with the look of a head full of unspoken words. Drew still had doubt etched all over his mind.

"Mark my words, Drew. I'm going to keep it real with you, Drew, you know you been my lor nigga for years and I got nothing but love for you. This anger ain't for us, Blair stole on Santana on some hoe shit. So, believe me when I tell you that lor nigga Blair will be doing a lot of fighting. While you playing... he better keep that tone on him," Tijuana managed to say as she put their leg irons on.

"Ma, look... I'm good. It's not that serious. I will handle me, believe that." Santana looked down at her as she put his shackles on. He wanted her to know he was sure of his words.

One thing he knew for sure, he couldn't let the disrespect slide. *In due time,* he promised himself. He looked at Drew. *What's understood doesn't need to be explained.*

The transport van had finally arrived. Still with nowhere to go, Clinton Hall was still in the gymnasium. Daylight still shone through the gym's stained-glass windows. The activities only hours before were still taking place as if nothing happened. *It was just another day in the Charles H. Hickey School,* he thought as he looked around. He laughed to himself. *You gotta love it.*

Shift had changed already, and Tijuana was on her way out. Santana watched as she talked to C.O. Underwood and another staff member he had never seen before. Santana stayed close to Drew, the fact that no one would look him in his eyes said enough. He had no love for them other niggas on the unit. Santana just stopped paying attention to them all together. *Who cares what how these fake-ass niggas feel?* He shrugged. *Not me.* Santana and Drew were seated at the far end of the stage that overlooked the gym. The stage was tucked in the back of the gym, away from everything. They both sat and observed the scenery. No words were exchanged between the two, none was needed. They knew what it was.

Santana watched Tijuana strut over to them. "Look, baby boy, I'm out, you make sure you keep yourself out of any trouble. At least until I come back tomorrow. Blair will be gone for a couple of weeks due to a broken jaw, so the infirmary is his new home until his shit heals up." She laughed. "That's what he gets." Tijuana turned and looked at Drew.

"Dre, I know I don't got to say this, but please watch over my baby. I will bring y'all some chicken boxes tomorrow when I come back. I'm not playing, both of you lor niggas better stay out of trouble while I'm gone." All three of them smiled.

"T, this my lor nigga too, I don't need no chicken box to ride for shorty. But don't forget that fruit punch half and half." Drew grinned as he grabbed Santana's shoulder.

"Yo, son! Y'all muthafuckas keep calling me a lil' nigga and we all will box," Santana replied. He had a little man's complex out of this world. He hated when people mistook his size for a weakness, even though at the moment that wasn't the case. Tijuana looked at Santana.

"Whatever, lor *nigga.*" Tijuana joked as Santana glared at her. Drew was having a good time looking at the two go at it.

"Bye y'all and remember what I said, stay out of trouble please." Tijuana nodded and went to walk off, leaving for the day.

"T!" Drew called after her. Tijuana turned around.

"Yo, tell your brother to shoot that shit through to me and stop bullshitting. Don't forget to holla at him when you get home, please T."

"I got you Drew. I have to go to Washington Park today anyway. That lor nigga supposed to be dropping money off for Mom. But I got you," Tijuana replied.

"Good looking for real shorty. Tell my nigga I said what's crackin' too." Tijuana rolled her eyes. She hated the fact that her brother was a part of a gang. It made no sense to her.

"I got you. Again, be safe, I'll see you tomorrow."

Santana sat here curiously thinking about the conversation that had just taken place in front of him. His mind seemed to be playing on his emotions. The conversation would mean nothing to anyone else, but it raised a set of questions for him, the question of loyalty. He didn't want to speak on the thoughts that ran through his head, but they were eating at him.

"Son, I thought you told me you weren't from Baltimore." Santana looked at Drew, confused.

For the Love of Blood

"I'm not, never lived in the city a day of my life. I'm from the county and I'm proud to admit that. I already told you where I'm from, shorty. I'm an Aberdeen nigga, shorty. Why you say that though? Speak what's on your mind." Santana instantly felt foolish.

"I always assumed Tijuana was from the city."

"Nah, shorty from around the way. I was raised with her family. Tijuana not that much older than me. Her lor brother my left-hand man, he a lor Crip nigga from Deen I grew up under."

"Oh yeah, that's what's up," Santana replied. He didn't know what to say. He wasn't expecting that kind of response. *Her brother is a Crip?* That changed the game... or did it? Drew saw the look on his face and understood immediately, so he spoke his own peace.

"In my hood, lor yo, all they breed is blue. It's a lot of people from all types of hoods but they *all* wear blue. Tijuana hates that gang shit, that's why she turned her nose up at me before she left. She hates that shit with a passion, but she still takes care of her family. Shorty cool for real. No need to dwell on it though. T loves you, if you can't tell." Drew laughed trying to make Santana feel more comfortable. Drew wanted him to put his guard down. But to no avail.

"So, you Crip too?" Santana asked the most important question.

"No, lor yo, I'm not. But I hope if I was, the love would be the same. Being real doesn't come with the color you bang, shorty. That shit come built within. Bang for a cause, not because of the color, my nigga. I know what you like and what color your heart bleed, but none of that matters to me. You my lor brother and I fuck with you hard body. So please, no more about this gang shit. We are on the same side. Loyalty is everything shorty, and you got mine," Drew replied, looking Santana square in the eyes. Santana understood.

"Say no more. It's dropped and of course, the love would be the same. That you don't have to question. I already told you what it was," Santana replied, without breaking any eye contact.

As the day passed by, more and more people began to disappear from the gym. Nobody could go back to Clinton Hall until the fire department came and cleared the unit. Plus, all the soot had to be cleaned up. So, with that being decided, the administration came to the conclusion to just split the inmates up throughout the remaining housing units. For the people that were awaiting placement for the enhancement programs, they were divided between, King, Jackson, and Roosevelt Hall. Everybody else that was on detention status was sent to Mandela Hall, pending court.

Mandela Hall was usually for the younger inmate population and overall, it was a good unit. It was less hostile, so it had fewer fights, and of course had fewer issues within its walls. Santana and Drew were moved to Unit 1 Mandella Hall. Santana thought about why Tijuana had taken such a liking to him. At first, he thought it was because he kept his mouth shut about the fight and the drugs, but it had to be more to it than that. The love they had for one another was too profound. You would have thought they popped out the same woman. It wasn't sexual. it didn't feel like it at least. Plus, he was too young for her. *Or was he?* The thoughts that paraded his mind were crazy. Whatever the connection. he was grateful for it. He let the thought go as he made his way into Mandela with the rest of the remaining inmates.

"Where everybody at, son?" Santana whispered to Drew.

For the Love of Blood

"I think it's lights out, lor yo, I'm not sure. We have been in the gym all day. It's different over here than Clinton Hall, different kind of niggas for real. Mandela ran on some family orientated shit. They get it crackin' though, just not on that unit 3 level. This is where you should have been anyway when you first came through the door. All the youngins get housed over here. I guess it'll be straight," Drew explained.

"You keep talking about young, nigga, how old are you?" Santana asked, knowing Drew couldn't be that much older than him.

"Sixteen in the life we live, that's not young, especially when you grow up in this hell hole," Drew answered.

"How old is Tijuana's brother?" Santana wanted to know. Maybe it could explain why she took such a liking to him.

"Shorty like eighteen now. I'm not sure, he at least about to turn eighteen, if he isn't already. The lor nigga about his money, but he never had to do this though." Drew raised his arms. He was talking of the notion that Mandella Hall offered. Drew continued. "He a good dude. I know you gone like him whenever y'all meet." That was the moment Santana understood that *lor nigga* was another form of Baltimore slang. It was crazy how different the slang changed when you went hours up the highway. New York City was only three hours away from Baltimore City, but everything about the two cities was totally different.

"That's what's good. You speak highly of son, so I can only imagine the loyalty you hold for each other," he stated.

"Vasquez! Cell 4, A side... " Mr. Underwood called out. Santana waited around to see what cell Drew would be put in. Drew was also put on side A, only a couple of doors down from his. Mr. Underwood finished calling out the rest of the inmates' new housing areas. When everyone found out what room they would be in, they moved to the back hallway in a pack.

Santana observed the surroundings of Unit 1. There were no cages whatsoever on Mandela. There was nothing that separated the gym from the day room. It was a tell-tale sign of a way more laid-back environment. It put Santana at ease. He hoped he would be able to see Tijuana while he was over on Mandella. But little did he know, Tijuana was the reason he and Drew was even on Mandela Hall, instead of Fort Hall, the committed unit. She also made sure she had a spot on their staff before she left the building that day. When Santana and Drew finally made it to the front of their doors, they dapped up and said their peace.

"Aight shorty," Drew said before he locked in. Santana nodded his head and continued down the hall to his new cell. When he walked into his room, a brown-skinned kid was sitting up reading *The Coldest Winter Ever*. He looked up as the door shut.

"What's good, dog?" the boy sat up straight. Santana laughed at his accent when he said *dog*. He had been hearing it for a while, but it still amazed him how they got *"Doug"* out of dog. He would probably never understand how.

"What's good, my G?" Santana replied as he put his valuables on the top bunk.

"What's your name, lor yo?"

"Santana." The kid laughed his own laugh this time.

"What's so funny, son?"

"You the lor nigga that everybody keeps saying burned the nigga Jimdog." Santana's demeanor changed.

"How does everybody know that shit? Is the city that small? And how does everybody know him?" These were the questions he had been waiting to ask, he just never came across the right person to ask.

For the Love of Blood

"Jimdog was just up here not too long ago. He was only on the streets a couple of months before he was shot. I grew up around the boy. He from my hood, but me and shorty were never cool, because he does too much showing off. I liked the nigga at times, but... it's just too hard to explain. Look, that shit y'all lor niggas got going on ain't got shit to do with me. Especially after I heard he put his hands on your raise.

"There aren't too many people over here that can stand that idiot. He from over East and he barely gets love from us. He a grimy kind of *nigga* for real. We call it O.F.S. That means *out for self.* Can't fuck with no one of that caliber when you out here in the midst of playing the game of the streets." Santana knew nothing about Jimdog, so all he could do was listen and take in as much information as possible.

"I didn't know the nigga myself, but he disrespected my lady. What's ya name, my G?"

"Glen, my dudes, but all my niggas call me Geezy. I'm from Jefferson and Rose, East Baltimore," Santana noticed the pride Geezy's voice held.

"That's what's up."

"You should like it over here. Laid back most of the time. If muthafuckas do get into it, they shoot the fair one. None of that banking shit y'all Clinton Hall niggas used to. Don't get me wrong, it happens, just not often."

"I hear that, I'm good. I did enough fighting to last me a while." Santana laughed.

"Heard all about you, what they say is you have heart. Especially for a young nigga with the odds stacked against him, I respect ya G." Geezy smiled.

"That's what's good, son. I'm tired as shit. today was a wild day. My face hurts, I need to lay down and catch some sleep. I'm about to hit this bunk. I'll fuck with you in the a.m." Santana made his bed.

"Aight, lor yo." Geezy got up and banged on the door for the night officers.

"Turn the light off for me please." The C.O. hit the light switch located on the outside of the door.

"Good looking, dog." Geezy went back to his bed and laid down. Santana was already halfway sleep by the time the lights went out. *Another day gone, another day closer to freedom,* he thought as he drifted into a deep sleep.

***

"Lor yo, wake up, they bout to serve breakfast. Make your bed too, they trip if your bed not made properly," Geezy explained to Santana as he made his own bed. Santana stirred at the sound of Glen's voice. He sat up as his head began to throb something awful. He had a mean ass headache. The side of his face was swollen from the events of the day before. His jaw felt as if it was out of place. He had to admit he was fucked up pretty bad.

Santana hopped down and made his way to the big bathroom so he could handle his hygiene. As he made the short trip, it felt like all eyes were on him. Santana waited his turn for a spot in the bathroom. When he finally made it inside the bathroom, he brushed his teeth, combed his hair and took a quick shower. He got out of the shower, feeling a little better than before. The hot water lessened his headache tremendously.

He walked back to his room to drop off his hygiene bag and rushed up front to the multi-purpose room for breakfast.

The sight was again different from the way things ran on Clinton Hall. Santana walked into the room and found a seat.

For the Love of Blood

He wasn't used to the family style atmosphere. On Unit 3, the multi-purpose room was boxed in with a cage, tables were placed everywhere, and tension was in the air at all times. But in Mandella, they had six picnic-like tables. Three tables were placed on each side of the spacious room. Everybody talked to each other, it was surprising. *Damn, that dumbass unit fucked my head up,* he thought as he looked at the different faces surrounding him. Santana was seated next to a light-skinned kid with nappy hair and gold teeth. The kid looked at him and nodded. He returned the gesture. Santana didn't make small talk. He ate, then went back to his cell.

He knew the routine, no matter what unit you were on. The staff as they liked to be called would be coming around soon to make sure everybody was ready for school. School at Hickey was a must. The Peabody School was where all the biggest fights took place. On the outside, the school looked like a bunch of connected trailers. The inside was a decently built school. They had just finished building the school only moments earlier and it was already known as a place of action.

Santana changed his clothes and walked down the hall to Drew's room. He looked inside but no one was there. He didn't remember seeing Drew at breakfast. He shrugged nonchalantly. Drew never ate breakfast, so it wasn't a red flag for him. Santana began the walk back up front to look for his Drew. No more than ten seconds later, Drew stormed past with a murderous look on his face. And if Santana wasn't tripping it looked like Drew had tears running down his face.

Drew's eyes were bloodshot and dazed.

"What's good son? Why you looking like that?" Santana asked with a worried look on his face. Drew didn't even acknowledge him and kept walking. Santana just watched Drew. When Drew got to his room, he slammed the door and hard as he could. Santana stood in the hallway dumbfounded.

What the fuck am I missing? he asked himself over and over again. He never saw Drew like that before. He didn't understand what he was missing, but he would try to find out. He walked to Drew's room and looked inside. Drew paced his room back and forth wiping the tears away from his eyes. It hurt Santana to see his friend like that. He did the only thing he knew to do, he opened the door.

"Son, what's poppin' with you? Why you acting like this?" he asked as he peered into the room.

"I'm good, shorty. Just for a minute, leave me to my thoughts. Please." Drew looked up with a tear-streaked face.

"But, son... " Santana tried to speak.

"Shorty, please." That was all Drew said before he started to pace the floor again. He gently pushed the door to the frame and walked off. He felt fucked up that he couldn't help Drew. As he made his way back to his cell, he saw Green walking towards him at a fast pace.

"Yo shorty, come fuck with me for a second. I need to holla at you." Santana looked at *him* with curiosity in his eyes.

"Aight, give me a second, let me tell bro..."

"Nah, lor yo fucked up right now over some other shit. Let him work out his issues." He looked at Green, then back at the back hallway. He chose his better judgment and walked off with C.O. Green. A lot of things ran through his mind as he took his seat in the counselor's office. Green sat behind the desk and handed him the phone. Santana's heart dropped. He knew it was the call that would shatter his life forever. He couldn't fathom his mother being gone. Santana let his emotions get the best of him. He didn't want to hear any bad news. He tried to hand the phone back to Green. Green looked at him confusingly; he didn't know what was wrong with Santana. He didn't understand why the little nigga was crying and he hadn't talked to anybody yet.

"It's Tijuana, lor yo, why you trippin'?" Green whispered. Green looked at Santana all crazy eyed. Santana's eyes grew wide, he was embarrassed. He felt his face turn hot. He wiped what tears he had on his face away and put the receiver to his ear.

"What's up, ma?"

"Hey, baby boy, how you holding up today? Is your face okay?" she asked through what sounded like her own sniffles.

"Tijuana, are you crying?" Santana asked Tijuana, looking up at Green for answers. Green looked away, breaking eye contact.

"Santana, I'm okay. Just an issue in the family. Look, I won't be back for like a week. I have a lot of things to handle out here," Tijuana explained.

"What's wrong, ma, don't just leave me in the dark. It's a reason I'm sitting on the other end of this phone. And to only be honest, I don't think it was to tell me you would be off for a week. So please, ma, talk to me." Tijuana started to cry uncontrollably. He let her cry, when she was ready, she would speak. Between Tijuana and Drew, he was losing his mind.

"Ba...by... I... Hold on... " He could hear her in the background trying to get herself together, she came back to the receiver and sighed.

"I'm sorry, baby, but I'm fucked up right now. My lor brother was killed the night before last. That shit... " she couldn't even finish her sentence. He knew her words couldn't explain the way she was feeling. Shit, he was lost for words his damn self. He didn't know the right words to say to comfort her, so he didn't try. All he could think was *damn*, but that wasn't what came out of his mouth.

"I'm sorry, T." They sat on the phone in silence for what seemed like forever.

"Santana?" He was lost in his own thoughts. "Santana, you still there?" Tijuana called out again.

"Yeah, I'm here, ma. I'll always be here. My heart goes out to you and your familia. I can't imagine that kind of loss. I almost lost my mother, and you were here for me, so you already know, ma. I got you when you need my ear. I love you, beautiful, always know that." It even surprised him the second he said it. Whether he wanted to admit it or not, he knew he meant every word. The conversation got silent again.

"Do you mean that or is it because of the pain you hear in my voice?"

"Ma, I mean what I say. I put that on Simfany."

"I love you too, Tana. Always have."

"Aight with all that mushy shit, my G." He laughed, hoping she would also. She did.

"Boy, you silly. I needed that though. How is Drew holding up?" Tijuana asked. He began putting two and two together. *Oh, shit....* he thought. *Son just lost his man and Tijuana lost her brother, damn...*

"He still fucked up. He's not talking to no one right now. Not even me. Now that I've talked to you, I understand better. Now I'm guessing it's your brother that has bro in his feelings."

"Yeah, they grew up around each other. Drew was like a lor brother to my family. I knew he would take it hard," Tijuana explained.

"Did they catch the person or people that killed him?" Santana asked.

"Yeah, he's probably getting processed now. He a young nigga too, so he might come through there. And believe me, if he do, he will come through Mandella for sure. The only thing is when I come back, they will most likely move him out of jail. Tell Drew to make sure he does that bitch ass nigga dirty.

Please because I don't want to see that nigga when I come back."

"Tijuana, say no more. We got you."

"No, you stay the fuck out of trouble. Have Drew handle his, he'll be okay."

"I know that's right. I'm forever riding, ma. I love you so that's what it is and what it's going to be. *We* got you, ma."

"Okay, Tana. Hold your head also. I will have Green bring you and Drew them chicken boxes later. I love you, baby boy," Tijuana said.

"I love you too, ma. I meant what I said, get your mind right. Me and Drew will be okay. Make sure you send son our way if you can."

"Okay, bye."

"Hold up, T, what's the dude's name that killed your brother?"

"Narvel Harris," Tijuana replied.

"That's what they call the nigga?" Santana asked as he frowned his face up to how corny the name sounded.

"Nah, they call the lor nigga Blaze."

"Okay, we got you. Get some rest, beautiful."

"Okay. Bye baby." Santana hung up the phone. C.O. Green looked at him and shook his head.

"Got a lot on ya plate huh?" Green asked.

"I'll be alright, nothing I can't handle. Thank you for the call. It put a lot of shit in place for me, because to be honest, I was clueless on what was going on around me."

"Let me ask you a question, shorty, why did you start crying before I handed you the phone? It seemed like you sensed death."

"I did, but I thought it was someone calling about my mother. She got shot a couple months back, thought they were calling me to bury my lady," Santana explained as they both walked out the counselor's office. The look on his face told Santana that he understood better. Santana continued...

"Plus, I didn't know that you could use them phones to call out. So, I really thought some fucked-up shit."

"I can see why you acted like that once I tried to hand you the phone. On Clinton Hall, they don't get to use the phones like that. All they do is wanna beef with each other. Look if you need to holla at someone just let me know. I'm here if you need me." Santana nodded. As he made his way back to his room, he noticed his room was empty. He jumped on his bunk to process his current situation. *All I have to do is stay out of trouble and I can go home in nine months.* He was in a fucked-up position. He knew what was best, but he was always going against his better judgment. Santana knew it was going to be ugly real soon. The hate he had bottled up inside would soon be released. He thought about the person that killed Tijuana's brother.

Blaze... Blaze... Blaze... I know I heard that name before but from where? he asked himself over and over. He came up blank. One thing was sure, and two things were for certain, Blaze wouldn't be able to live in the same complex with Drew and Santana.

Chapter 12

The blaring phone woke Simfany out of her sleep. *Who the fuck could this be? I'm going to kill Carol,* she thought. She looked at the clock that sat on the nightstand next to her bed. *It's 4:15 a.m., are you fucking kidding me?* Simfany pulled the pillow over her head and waited for the phone to quit ringing. It stopped then started again. Simfany sighed and picked the phone up.

"This shit better be good," Simfany said in a groggy voice.

"I want to see you," the man on the other end replied.

"Who is this?" She recognized the voice but couldn't place it.

"Carlos." They both fell silent.

"How did you get my number?" She was scared to death, and he could hear it in her voice.

"Fuerza, Chula, fuerza," he spoke in his native tongue.

"Papi, speak English please. I understand little. Why do you want to see me?"

"We have business to attend to, no? You're in no harm, beautiful, my word. I just need a minute of your time." Carlos sounded sincere.

"When and where, Carlos?" She knew she didn't really have a choice once he asked. He would get what we wanted regardless. Simfany was now fully awake. As she waited for a response, she made her way into the bathroom. She knew it was no going back to sleep after a phone call like this. His name alone could make a fiend go cold turkey.

"Now, Chula." He hung up. Seconds after the phone disconnected, the sound of a car horn beeped outside her window. Simfany combed her hair and brushed her teeth before she made her way out the door to an awaiting Carlos.

As Simfany approached the car, the driver's side door opened and out got a huge, Spanish looking man.

"I apologize, Ms. Vasquez, but it's a must that you must be searched." Simfany put her hands on top of her head and what seemed to be Carlos's bodyguard searched her person. The man did his best not to violate her. When he was finally finished, he stated, "I apologize you had to go through that, but I hope you understand." He opened the door to an awaiting Carlos. As Simfany got into the car, she realized Carlos wasn't as old as she assumed.

"Please get comfortable. Juan, drive around a little bit. Get used to these streets," Carlos stated to his henchman. He looked over and admired Simfany's beauty.

"Not to be rude, Carlos, but I do not understand the meaning of this visit. Too many people don't get to see your face, and if they do, it's likely they never will be seen again. So, what's the pleasure?" Simfany asked.

"I'm here about Byrd and some other reasons." Simfany's heart dropped at the mention of Byrd's name. *Does he really think I had something to do with Byrd's death?*

"What about him, Carlos? There's nothing more I can tell you then you already know." Carlos looked at Simfany and gave her a smile worth a million dollars.

"I don't think you killed Byrd, sweetheart. I know you didn't even know about what happened to Byrd, but that's only one half of the reason that I'm here tonight. I understand you called a number recently and you asked for help, am I right?" Carlos waited for an answer.

"What are you talking about?" she asked cluelessly.

"Chula, please. You are in no harm, but you remember the number Dracula gave you almost fourteen years earlier." That stopped Simfany's breathing altogether. *How the fuck do this nigga know about Dracula and the number he gave me?* She

For the Love of Blood

thought hard. *Nah, there's no way.* She tried to convince herself, but she knew that power came with resources.

"What does that number have to do with anything?" she asked him.

"A lot, mami, a lot." She thought back to the day she dialed the number that was up for question. The person on the other line that had picked up simply said, "I'll be there." Simfany had no clue who the voice belonged to. Dracula had given her the number in case of an emergency. Years had passed by, and she never needed to use the number, but when she was shot Simfany felt her back was against the wall, she had no choice. She didn't expect the number to still be a working number because of the time that had passed. But the number was still active, and this meeting was the product of that call.

"To ease your mind, let me explain. I know you and your family's whole background. I do now at least. I know what bodies you dropped and why. The number you called is a longtime friend of mine that was very close to your child's father. It breaks my heart that I'm one of the reasons that you may have been harmed. I didn't directly send anyone to harm you, but my actions alone started this mayhem. I let my emotions get me into a war I had no business taking a part in. Byrd was like a son to me, yes, he killed for me, but I gave him everything. The bricks you gave him turned him into somebody I never knew.

"But that's not your fault he let the money change him. Money does that sometimes. It was the disloyalty that came in between me and Byrd. His little money making led to our misunderstanding. He chose the love of money over the loyalty he once possessed for me. Even though he said he didn't, his eyes told a different story."

Carlos sighed.

"Long story short, he bit the hand that was trying to feed him. After shots were fired, I pulled back. I knew Byrd couldn't get to me, so I let go of the *beef*. I couldn't be the reason for Byrd's demise. So, I was the bigger man and waved the white flag. But what I did do was cut all ties with him once the war was over. I gave him my one and only blessing. The reason I tell you all this, is because I think I know who killed him." Instead of asking the obvious question, she sat there and waited for him to continue.

"I believe Jimdog killed Byrd. I can't explain exactly why I feel like that right now, but I have a strong feeling that Jimdog killed his brother." Carlos pulled on the cigar he had in the corner of his mouth. Simfany sat and took all the information in.

"So, that's why you're looking for Jimdog?" she thought out loud.

"Yeah, well kind of. I'm not looking to do nothing to him yet, but there is a lot that needs to be explained. I'm not stressing him or this issue, your safety is my main concern. My bodyguard here has a twin with the same training. He can be your bodyguard if you want, to what extent of protection is solely up to you, Simfany." Carlos saw the look Simfany held on her face when he began to explain about the bodyguard situation.

"Carlos…"

"Look Chula, know he's only a call away if you need him. He won't be around forever, so use him while the opportunity presents itself. He will be around until this Baltimore situation is over with. This is my question to you, why haven't you attempted to move yet?"

"My son," Simfany simply stated, summing it all up in two easy words.

For the Love of Blood

"Ahhh, I understand. I like him very much. To protect his familia is big where I grew up, especially to protect your madre. Big heart he has. A trait from his pa, no?"

"Yeah, Dracula held the same trait," Simfany said sadly, but with a heart filled with gratitude. She missed Dracula so much, with Santana it seemed like she was raising him. Santana reminded her so much of his father, from his looks to the way he carried himself. It was as if Dracula spit the little nigga out himself. Simfany knew Santana would most likely be a handful once he was released from Juvie. She couldn't understand his everyday struggle. He went from the son of a hood legend and everybody from his borough knowing him, to fighting every day and being alone at the end of the night. Simfany tried to understand but she knew it would be impossible.

"Well, you just call this number if you feel like you're in trouble. I'm hoping we never have to *see* each other on these terms again, so please take care of yourself, beautiful. Start telling your son the truth, he deserves it. But again, if you need to, use the number. Simfany, to be more on the safe side, stay strapped as you call it, you know what it is out there right now. Nobody's untouchable. You never know who hates you out here in these streets, Chula." Carlos looked up front at his bodyguard.

"Juan, pull back up in front of Ms. Vasquez's home please."

"Thank you, Carlos." Simfany exited the car as Juan stood holding the door.

"You have a nice day, Ms. Vasquez and be careful." Juan closed the door and made his way back to the driver's side. Within seconds the car was gone, leaving Simfany standing there with only her thoughts. *Only if she knew how powerful Dracula had been, he was a well-respected man, that's for sure.* She came to that conclusion only a few minutes ago. Her thoughts ran wild as she made her way back inside, leaving the cold air and the fear of death on the sidewalk. What bothered Simfany was the possibility of Jimdog killing Byrd, that revelation was astonishing. *But why?* she questioned. *What would be the point? None of this makes sense,* but as she thought of scenarios and reasons why. Simfany's mind seemed to be playing the same song, no matter how much she twisted or turned it. The truth was the truth. And she believes her truth was envy and the most common reason for betrayal, money.

Money was truly the root of all evil when it came to the human race, especially when you were raised in the streets. No one played fair when enough money is involved. For the love of money, the good in people turn sour. No matter what hood, what religion, what creed or what race, if the price was right anybody was liable to be harmed over them greenbacks. That was a language the dead knew all too well. So, it didn't come to Simfany as a surprise when she thought about the power struggle between the two brothers.

The meeting Simfany held with Carlos helped her sleep more peacefully. She no longer had to worry about him and his power reaching her. She was safe, or so she thought. What she didn't know was the danger she was putting herself in. Even though she thought she was in a *new* environment, she was very well still familiar to the pack of wolves, ready to kill at any time. The streets, no matter where she went or whose blessings she had, were watching.

Detective Lawson sat outside of Carol Washington's apartment for several weeks to observe Simfany's movement. Ramos was so satisfied with the "she won't tell" bullshit that he sat on his ass and did nothing. Lawson knew it was more to the story. The connection was too deep, and both sides proved to be dangerous. Only if he knew how deep it would truly get, he would stay away. Lawson knew to get to the core, he would have to find out the cause of Byrd's death, and he knew the rest would unfold.

As Detective Lawson sipped on his late-night coffee, he saw a black town car pull into the HillTop residence. At first the black car just sat there, raising questions. Lawson looked down at the dash clock and it read 4:15 a.m. *Who could this be running around here at this time of the hour?* He questioned. It didn't surprise him when Simfany came out of the home. The surprise came seconds later when Lawson recognized the face of Juan Santiago.

The Santiago brothers were known to the Baltimore police and FBI as being the hired hands for Carlos Rivera. He watched as Juan searched Simfany before she entered the car.

Lawson put his coffee down and picked up his folder that he kept with him regarding the Parks and Vasquez connections. He pulled out the paper that had names and lines drawn on them. The sheet was of everybody connected to Simfany Vasquez and Brian "Byrd" Parks. He smiled as he drew a line from Carlos to Simfany forever connecting the two in the eyes of the law.

"Romeo will never believe this shit," said Lawson, as he jotted notes in his folder. He couldn't believe his luck. The promotion he saw coming made him excited as hell.

Detective Lawson put the folder on the passenger seat and put the car in gear. The excitement he was feeling faded as a black figure emerged from the shadows holding a modified assault rifle.

"Wait! I—"

The Reaper opened fire, cutting off Lawson's plea.

To Be Continued...

Jamel Mitchell

For the Love of Blood 2
Comin Soon

Author's Last Thoughts

I was inspired to write this book because of the loyalty issues in the streets. I hope to give the message of being aware of who you love and trust. Because we never really know what people's intentions are until it's too late. The streets play for keeps, no matter who the player is, or how good the player plays. Your friends are your worst enemy, they know all the weaknesses you have. So, I inspire all the people that take time out to read this series to remain loyal to yourself, before you can remain loyal to another.

For any questions or comments write ...

Jamel K. Mitchell # 3468987
Huttonsville Correctional Center
P.O. Box 1
Huttonsville, WV 26273

Lock Down Publications and Ca$h Presents assisted publishing packages.

BASIC PACKAGE $499

Editing

Cover Design

Formatting

UPGRADED PACKAGE $800

Typing

Editing

Cover Design

Formatting

ADVANCE PACKAGE $1,200

Typing

Editing

Cover Design

Formatting

Copyright registration

Proofreading

For the Love of Blood

Upload book to Amazon

LDP SUPREME PACKAGE $1,500

Typing

Editing

Cover Design

Formatting

Copyright registration

Proofreading

Set up Amazon account

Upload book to Amazon

Advertise on LDP Amazon and Facebook page

***Other services available upon request. Additional charges may apply

Lock Down Publications

P.O. Box 944

Stockbridge, GA 30281-9998

Phone # 470 303-9761

Jamel Mitchell

Submission Guideline

Submit the first three chapters of your completed manuscript to ldpsubmissions@gmail.com, subject line: Your book's title. The manuscript must be in a .doc file and sent as an attachment. Document should be in Times New Roman, double spaced and in size 12 font. Also, provide your synopsis and full contact information. If sending multiple submissions, they must each be in a separate email.

Have a story but no way to send it electronically? You can still submit to LDP/Ca$h Presents. Send in the first three chapters, written or typed, of your completed manuscript to:

LDP: Submissions Dept
Po Box 944
Stockbridge, Ga 30281

DO NOT send original manuscript. Must be a duplicate.

Provide your synopsis and a cover letter containing your full contact information.

Thanks for considering LDP and Ca$h Presents.

NEW RELEASES

THE BIRTH OF A GANGSTER by DELMONT PLAYER
MOB TIES 6 by SAYNOMORE
A GANGSTA'S PAIN 2 by J-BLUNT
TREAL LOVE by LE'MONICA JACKSON
FOR THE LOVE OF BLOOD by JAMEL MITCHELL

Jamel Mitchell

Coming Soon from Lock Down Publications/Ca$h Presents
BLOOD OF A BOSS **VI**
SHADOWS OF THE GAME II
TRAP BASTARD II
By **Askari**
LOYAL TO THE GAME **IV**
By **T.J. & Jelissa**
IF TRUE SAVAGE **VIII**
MIDNIGHT CARTEL IV
DOPE BOY MAGIC IV
CITY OF KINGZ III
NIGHTMARE ON SILENT AVE II
THE PLUG OF LIL MEXICO II
By **Chris Green**
BLAST FOR ME **III**
A SAVAGE DOPEBOY III
CUTTHROAT MAFIA III
DUFFLE BAG CARTEL VII
HEARTLESS GOON VI
By **Ghost**
A HUSTLER'S DECEIT III
KILL ZONE II
BAE BELONGS TO ME III
By **Aryanna**
KING OF THE TRAP III
By **T.J. Edwards**
GORILLAZ IN THE BAY V

For the Love of Blood

3X KRAZY III
STRAIGHT BEAST MODE II
De'Kari
KINGPIN KILLAZ IV
STREET KINGS III
PAID IN BLOOD III
CARTEL KILLAZ IV
DOPE GODS III
Hood Rich
SINS OF A HUSTLA II
ASAD
RICH $AVAGE II
By Martell Troublesome Bolden
YAYO V
Bred In The Game 2
S. Allen
CREAM III
THE STREETS WILL TALK II
By Yolanda Moore
SON OF A DOPE FIEND III
HEAVEN GOT A GHETTO II
By Renta
LOYALTY AIN'T PROMISED III
By Keith Williams
I'M NOTHING WITHOUT HIS LOVE II
SINS OF A THUG II
TO THE THUG I LOVED BEFORE II

Jamel Mitchell

IN A HUSTLER I TRUST II
By Monet Dragun
QUIET MONEY IV
EXTENDED CLIP III
THUG LIFE IV
By **Trai'Quan**
THE STREETS MADE ME IV
By **Larry D. Wright**
IF YOU CROSS ME ONCE II
By **Anthony Fields**
THE STREETS WILL NEVER CLOSE IV
By K'ajji
HARD AND RUTHLESS III
KILLA KOUNTY III
By Khufu
MONEY GAME III
By Smoove Dolla
JACK BOYS VS DOPE BOYS II
A GANGSTA'S QUR'AN V
COKE GIRLZ II
By Romell Tukes
MURDA WAS THE CASE II
Elijah R. Freeman
THE STREETS NEVER LET GO II
By Robert Baptiste
AN UNFORESEEN LOVE III
By **Meesha**

For the Love of Blood

KING OF THE TRENCHES III
by **GHOST & TRANAY ADAMS**

MONEY MAFIA II
LOYAL TO THE SOIL III
By **Jibril Williams**

QUEEN OF THE ZOO II
By **Black Migo**

THE BRICK MAN IV
By King Rio

VICIOUS LOYALTY III
By Kingpen

A GANGSTA'S PAIN III
By J-Blunt

CONFESSIONS OF A JACKBOY III
By Nicholas Lock

GRIMEY WAYS II
By Ray Vinci

KING KILLA II
By Vincent "Vitto" Holloway

BETRAYAL OF A THUG II
By Fre$h

THE MURDER QUEENS II
By Michael Gallon

THE BIRTH OF A GANGSTER II
By Delmont Player

TREAL LOVE II
By Le'Monica Jackson

Jamel Mitchell

FOR THE LOVE OF BLOOD II
By Jamel Mitchell

Available Now

RESTRAINING ORDER **I & II**
By **CA$H & Coffee**
LOVE KNOWS NO BOUNDARIES **I II & III**
By **Coffee**
RAISED AS A GOON I, II, III & IV
BRED BY THE SLUMS I, II, III
BLAST FOR ME I & II
ROTTEN TO THE CORE I II III
A BRONX TALE I, II, III
DUFFLE BAG CARTEL I II III IV V VI
HEARTLESS GOON I II III IV V
A SAVAGE DOPEBOY I II
DRUG LORDS I II III
CUTTHROAT MAFIA I II
KING OF THE TRENCHES
By **Ghost**
LAY IT DOWN **I & II**

For the Love of Blood

LAST OF A DYING BREED I II
BLOOD STAINS OF A SHOTTA I & II III
By **Jamaica**
LOYAL TO THE GAME I II III
LIFE OF SIN I, II III
By **TJ & Jelissa**
BLOODY COMMAS I & II
SKI MASK CARTEL I II & III
KING OF NEW YORK I II,III IV V
RISE TO POWER I II III
COKE KINGS I II III IV V
BORN HEARTLESS I II III IV
KING OF THE TRAP I II
By **T.J. Edwards**
IF LOVING HIM IS WRONG…I & II
LOVE ME EVEN WHEN IT HURTS I II III
By **Jelissa**
WHEN THE STREETS CLAP BACK I & II III
THE HEART OF A SAVAGE I II III
MONEY MAFIA
LOYAL TO THE SOIL I II
By **Jibril Williams**
A DISTINGUISHED THUG STOLE MY HEART I II & III
LOVE SHOULDN'T HURT I II III IV
RENEGADE BOYS I II III IV
PAID IN KARMA I II III
SAVAGE STORMS I II III

Jamel Mitchell

AN UNFORESEEN LOVE I II
By **Meesha**
A GANGSTER'S CODE I &, II III
A GANGSTER'S SYN I II III
THE SAVAGE LIFE I II III
CHAINED TO THE STREETS I II III
BLOOD ON THE MONEY I II III
A GANGSTA'S PAIN I II
By J-Blunt
PUSH IT TO THE LIMIT
By **Bre' Hayes**
BLOOD OF A BOSS **I, II, III, IV, V**
SHADOWS OF THE GAME
TRAP BASTARD
By **Askari**
THE STREETS BLEED MURDER **I, II & III**
THE HEART OF A GANGSTA I II& III
By **Jerry Jackson**
CUM FOR ME I II III IV V VI VII VIII
An **LDP Erotica Collaboration**
BRIDE OF A HUSTLA **I II & II**
THE FETTI GIRLS **I, II& III**
CORRUPTED BY A GANGSTA I, II III, IV
BLINDED BY HIS LOVE
THE PRICE YOU PAY FOR LOVE I, II ,III
DOPE GIRL MAGIC I II III
By **Destiny Skai**

For the Love of Blood

WHEN A GOOD GIRL GOES BAD
By **Adrienne**
THE COST OF LOYALTY I II III
By Kweli
A GANGSTER'S REVENGE **I II III & IV**
THE BOSS MAN'S DAUGHTERS I II III IV V
A SAVAGE LOVE **I & II**
BAE BELONGS TO ME I II
A HUSTLER'S DECEIT I, II, III
WHAT BAD BITCHES DO I, II, III
SOUL OF A MONSTER I II III
KILL ZONE
A DOPE BOY'S QUEEN I II III
By **Aryanna**
A KINGPIN'S AMBITON
A KINGPIN'S AMBITION **II**
I MURDER FOR THE DOUGH
By **Ambitious**
TRUE SAVAGE I II III IV V VI VII
DOPE BOY MAGIC I, II, III
MIDNIGHT CARTEL I II III
CITY OF KINGZ I II
NIGHTMARE ON SILENT AVE
THE PLUG OF LIL MEXICO II

By **Chris Green**
A DOPEBOY'S PRAYER

Jamel Mitchell

By **Eddie "Wolf" Lee**
THE KING CARTEL **I, II & III**
By **Frank Gresham**
THESE NIGGAS AIN'T LOYAL **I, II & III**
By **Nikki Tee**
GANGSTA SHYT **I II &III**
By **CATO**
THE ULTIMATE BETRAYAL
By **Phoenix**
BOSS'N UP **I , II & III**
By **Royal Nicole**
I LOVE YOU TO DEATH
By **Destiny J**
I RIDE FOR MY HITTA
I STILL RIDE FOR MY HITTA
By **Misty Holt**
LOVE & CHASIN' PAPER
By **Qay Crockett**
TO DIE IN VAIN
SINS OF A HUSTLA
By **ASAD**
BROOKLYN HUSTLAZ
By **Boogsy Morina**
BROOKLYN ON LOCK I & II
By **Sonovia**
GANGSTA CITY
By **Teddy Duke**

For the Love of Blood

A DRUG KING AND HIS DIAMOND I & II III
A DOPEMAN'S RICHES
HER MAN, MINE'S TOO I, II
CASH MONEY HO'S
THE WIFEY I USED TO BE I II
By **Nicole Goosby**
TRAPHOUSE KING **I II & III**
KINGPIN KILLAZ I II III
STREET KINGS I II
PAID IN BLOOD **I II**
CARTEL KILLAZ I II III
DOPE GODS I II
By **Hood Rich**
LIPSTICK KILLAH **I, II, III**
CRIME OF PASSION I II & III
FRIEND OR FOE I II III
By **Mimi**
STEADY MOBBN' **I, II, III**
THE STREETS STAINED MY SOUL I II III
By **Marcellus Allen**
WHO SHOT YA **I, II, III**
SON OF A DOPE FIEND I II
HEAVEN GOT A GHETTO
Renta
GORILLAZ IN THE BAY **I II III IV**
TEARS OF A GANGSTA I II
3X KRAZY I II

Jamel Mitchell

STRAIGHT BEAST MODE
DE'KARI
TRIGGADALE I II III
MURDAROBER WAS THE CASE
Elijah R. Freeman
GOD BLESS THE TRAPPERS I, II, III
THESE SCANDALOUS STREETS I, II, III
FEAR MY GANGSTA I, II, III IV, V
THESE STREETS DON'T LOVE NOBODY I, II
BURY ME A G I, II, III, IV, V
A GANGSTA'S EMPIRE I, II, III, IV
THE DOPEMAN'S BODYGAURD I II
THE REALEST KILLAZ I II III
THE LAST OF THE OGS I II III
Tranay Adams
THE STREETS ARE CALLING
Duquie Wilson
MARRIED TO A BOSS I II III
By Destiny Skai & Chris Green
KINGZ OF THE GAME I II III IV V VI
Playa Ray
SLAUGHTER GANG I II III
RUTHLESS HEART I II III
By Willie Slaughter
FUK SHYT
By Blakk Diamond
DON'T F#CK WITH MY HEART I II

For the Love of Blood

By Linnea
ADDICTED TO THE DRAMA I II III
IN THE ARM OF HIS BOSS II

By Jamila
YAYO I II III IV
A SHOOTER'S AMBITION I II
BRED IN THE GAME

By S. Allen
TRAP GOD I II III
RICH $AVAGE
MONEY IN THE GRAVE I II III

By Martell Troublesome Bolden
FOREVER GANGSTA
GLOCKS ON SATIN SHEETS I II

By Adrian Dulan
TOE TAGZ I II III IV
LEVELS TO THIS SHYT I II

By Ah'Million
KINGPIN DREAMS I II III

By Paper Boi Rari
CONFESSIONS OF A GANGSTA I II III IV
CONFESSIONS OF A JACKBOY I II

By Nicholas Lock
I'M NOTHING WITHOUT HIS LOVE
SINS OF A THUG
TO THE THUG I LOVED BEFORE
A GANGSTA SAVED XMAS

Jamel Mitchell

IN A HUSTLER I TRUST
By Monet Dragun
CAUGHT UP IN THE LIFE I II III
THE STREETS NEVER LET GO
By Robert Baptiste
NEW TO THE GAME I II III
MONEY, MURDER & MEMORIES I II III
By **Malik D. Rice**
LIFE OF A SAVAGE I II III
A GANGSTA'S QUR'AN I II III IV
MURDA SEASON I II III
GANGLAND CARTEL I II III
CHI'RAQ GANGSTAS I II III
KILLERS ON ELM STREET I II III
JACK BOYZ N DA BRONX I II III
A DOPEBOY'S DREAM I II III
JACK BOYS VS DOPE BOYS
COKE GIRLZ
By Romell Tukes
LOYALTY AIN'T PROMISED I II
By Keith Williams
QUIET MONEY I II III
THUG LIFE I II III
EXTENDED CLIP I II
By **Trai'Quan**
THE STREETS MADE ME I II III
By **Larry D. Wright**

For the Love of Blood

THE ULTIMATE SACRIFICE I, II, III, IV, V, VI
KHADIFI
IF YOU CROSS ME ONCE
ANGEL I II
IN THE BLINK OF AN EYE
By **Anthony Fields**
THE LIFE OF A HOOD STAR
By **Ca$h & Rashia Wilson**
THE STREETS WILL NEVER CLOSE I II III
By **K'ajji**
CREAM I II
THE STREETS WILL TALK
By **Yolanda Moore**
NIGHTMARES OF A HUSTLA I II III
By **King Dream**
CONCRETE KILLA I II
VICIOUS LOYALTY I II
By **Kingpen**
HARD AND RUTHLESS I II
MOB TOWN 251
THE BILLIONAIRE BENTLEYS I II III
By **Von Diesel**
GHOST MOB
Stilloan Robinson
MOB TIES I II III IV V VI
By **SayNoMore**
BODYMORE MURDERLAND I II III

Jamel Mitchell

THE BIRTH OF A GANGSTER
By Delmont Player
FOR THE LOVE OF A BOSS
By C. D. Blue
MOBBED UP I II III IV
THE BRICK MAN I II III
THE COCAINE PRINCESS I II III IV V
By King Rio
KILLA KOUNTY I II III
By Khufu
MONEY GAME I II
By Smoove Dolla
A GANGSTA'S KARMA I II
By FLAME
KING OF THE TRENCHES I II
by **GHOST & TRANAY ADAMS**
QUEEN OF THE ZOO
By **Black Migo**
GRIMEY WAYS
By Ray Vinci
XMAS WITH AN ATL SHOOTER
By Ca$h & Destiny Skai
KING KILLA
By Vincent "Vitto" Holloway
BETRAYAL OF A THUG
By Fre$h
THE MURDER QUEENS

For the Love of Blood

By Michael Gallon
TREAL LOVE
By Le'Monica Jackson
FOR THE LOVE OF BLOOD
By Jamel Mitchell

Jamel Mitchell

BOOKS BY LDP'S CEO, CA$H

TRUST IN NO MAN
TRUST IN NO MAN 2
TRUST IN NO MAN 3
BONDED BY BLOOD
SHORTY GOT A THUG
THUGS CRY
THUGS CRY 2
THUGS CRY 3
TRUST NO BITCH
TRUST NO BITCH 2
TRUST NO BITCH 3
TIL MY CASKET DROPS
RESTRAINING ORDER
RESTRAINING ORDER 2
IN LOVE WITH A CONVICT
LIFE OF A HOOD STAR
XMAS WITH AN ATL SHOOTER

For the Love of Blood

CPSIA information can be obtained
at www.ICGtesting.com
Printed in the USA
LVHW020618270722
724372LV00013B/388